RIDICULOUSLY ROYAL

COLLECTION

KATE TILNEY

SARAH

RIDICULOUSLY ROYAL #1

ONE

SARAH

Masking a yawn, I slip into the throne room. Nodding to my younger brother Alex, I take an empty seat with one minute to spare.

While most kings have used the throne room for official events—such as investitures and proclamations—my father, King Reginald II of Rhodon, uses it for even the most mundane of family meetings. He says he likes the natural light that comes in through the East-facing windows. Mother says he loves the drama of sitting on a gold chair while he looks down on everyone.

I cover my mouth to hide another yawn as my twin brother, Henry, sits next to me, unbuttoning his suit coat in a swift motion as he does.

"I hope you were not up all night partying again." He smirks. "I believe dancing on tabletops would be conduct unbecoming of the future queen of Rhodon."

Despite what the press says, I have never danced on a table in my life. I could tell my brother I was up half the night studying our country's constitution and history. But what would be the fun in that? "It's only my first week on the job. I am bound to slip up."

"Mmm." He nods, his dark brown eyes sparkling with amusement. "I have so much to learn about being the spare to the heir."

"I could give you a few pointers any time you like. But I imagine you will be a natural."

"One can hope."

It's nice we can joke about this. I imagine others in our position—even in our family tree—might not be able to find humor in the situation.

Last week when word broke that high-ranking officials in the government and household had lied about our birth order twenty-six years ago, we had naturally been shocked. A week before Henry and I were born, our grandfather had changed the law so that the firstborn child—not the firstborn male—would-be heir. Not everyone had been on board with modernization.

Since we were literally born behind a curtain in an operating room, it had been easy for the paid-off doctors to lie to our parents and the world. They probably would have gotten away with it if one of the doctors had not suddenly grown a conscience. After more evidence surfaced to support his claim, the palace went into crisis mode. Meetings were held. People fired. Criminal charges ordered.

And now, one day I will be queen and my brother—who trained for the job his whole life—will not.

"You know," I say, studying my nails, which could use a fresh coat of paint, "I could always abdicate."

"We have been over this. I am afraid we both have too much duty and honor in our veins to do that."

He might, but I am not so sure about myself.

Though he has not said it, based on how cheerful he has been this week, I suspect Henry is more than happy to give up the job. Lucky bastard.

Before I can use my best, most annoying, sister tone to beg, our father enters the room followed by our mother.

He frowns. "Where is James?"

"Here, Father." He saunters in through the door. "I was finishing up a meeting with an ambassador."

"Is that what they are calling lingerie models these days?" Henry mutters under his breath.

Alex snorts but pulls his shoulders up and back when Father glares at him.

Still sporting a smirk, James plops down next to Alex. If they didn't have the same face, you would hardly guess they were identical twins. One the perfect soldier. The other, Casanova in the flesh.

James crosses an ankle over his knee. "What's this all about, Pops?"

Clearing his throat, Father sits rigidly in his throne, every inch the king. I could practice for hours, and I'd never look so clearly in command.

"I do not need to rehash the situation at hand. We have gone over that already. And even if we had not, I doubt you could have missed it."

Mother sighs. "The international press corps has run away with this whole scandal."

"Not a scandal. Situation." Trust Father to put a lifetime of public relations to work in a private family conversation. "Now, the issue is how we must act. Our new advisor"—his word for crisis manager—"suggests everyone resumes normal activities. Immediately."

James perks up. "Am I to return to Cambridge then?"

Father nods, and James fist pumps. "Alex, you will rejoin your regiment."

Though he does not respond, there is no denying the relief on his face. Alex has never particularly enjoyed sticking around the palace longer than a holiday.

"Your mother and I will return to our regular appearances and schedules."

That leaves only Henry and me without our marching orders. Unlike everyone else in this room, there is no going back to normal for us.

At last, Father says, "Henry, I would like you to spend some time in London."

Henry arches an eyebrow. "Am I to be banished, then?"

Mother rests a hand on Father's forearm before he can reply. "Of course not darling. Our advisor simply believes it might be best to . . . keep you out of public view during the transition."

"Sounds like banishment to me," Henry whispers for my ears only, before clearing his throat and speaking louder. "When do I leave?"

"You three will leave in the morning." Father turns his stare toward me. "As for you, as the future Queen of Rhodon, there are certain expectations of you."

From there he runs through a list of my new job duties as a queen in training. First, there are my private tutoring sessions in everything from the role our sovereign plays in government to how I properly knight a person. Then, I will need to add on to my list of charities. And if that was not enough, I will be expected to make appearances at the opera, ballet, and a handful of other dignified evening outings this week.

A dull ache forms behind my eyes just thinking about it.

There goes my social life. Before I can ask Father when I will have a chance to eat, sleep, or schedule a nail appointment, he holds up his hand.

"There is one more matter. It is about your safety." His tone takes on an edge sharp enough that even James's smirk slips from his lips. "As the future queen, it will be necessary to increase your security detail. Particularly these next few months."

Alex's eyebrows shoot up. "Have there been threats?"

"Nothing serious or concrete. However, I am afraid that there are a number of our residents who have yet to embrace the notion of a future queen."

"Probably the same jerks behind this whole mess to begin with," James says, with a nod of agreement from Alex.

"In light of these . . . tense emotions, I have hired a private security officer to accompany you at all times in the interim."

My jaw drops. This seems a little over the top. Especially if there have not been any threats. Though, the idea of a possible threat does put ice in my veins.

"No shit." James chuckles. "You get your own bodyguard?"

"Security detail," Father corrects. "He comes highly recommended by his agency. Served tours in Iraq and Afghanistan as well as several covert operations for the U.S. government."

"An American?" Alex frowns. "Were our soldiers not good enough?"

"He works for an international agency that specializes in high profile clients." Father gives Alex a silencing look before turning back to me. "I have arranged for you to meet him this afternoon."

"Are you sure this is absolutely necessary?" I ask. "I do not see a need for a hired shadow with a gun."

"Protecting the life of the future sovereign is of the utmost importance. I expect you all to do as you have been told. It is your duty to bring honor to our family and country."

TWO

RYAN

Who does a guy have to screw to get a cup of coffee around this place?

Only years of training in the roughest conditions keep me from yawning or itching at the collar of the dark black suit I have been given to wear. Working in private security for the rich and famous, I've worn my share of uniforms for the job. But the heavy wool fabric of this overpriced palace-issued suit might be the worst yet.

Then again, that could just be the jet-lag talking.

My new boss Georgio, a middle-aged man with pencil-thin mustache and shocks of silver hair above his ears, clears his throat.

"Shall we go over the royals, their titles, and forms of address one more time?"

"I'm good."

His eyes narrow. "You seem awfully sure of yourself."

"I am."

I spent the flight from Seattle studying the Bible-sized dossier the palace had sent. It included a family tree dating back to the Middle Ages, and a list of royal protocol, including when I must bow—and for how long—to each member of the household. It had several chapters on my charge: the crowned princess herself. I know her charities, her ex-boyfriends, and every bar she's set foot in. And I know that she's a looker with a bit of sass.

A princess with an attitude. Go figure.

Georgio's mustache twitches. "Your agency told us that you would bring a firearm."

"I did." Opening the coat, I reveal a Glock 22 in a holster. I lift my pant leg to show a Ruger. "I also have a few other pieces in the safe in my room."

"Very well. We'll need you to provide a full list including makes, serial numbers and—"

His order dies on his lips as I fish into my pocket and hand him a complete registry of every weapon I've brought.

His dark eyebrows shoot up and I smirk.

"My agency has a sterling reputation for a reason. Your king asked for the best. They've sent you the best."

"Humble too, it would seem."

I lift a shoulder. I could pretend I don't come highly decorated with both military and civilian honors. I've earned every accolade I have. I don't exactly go around spouting off my credentials, but I'm not going to play coy either.

"Are there any updates on my client?"

Georgio gestures for me to take a seat. He slides a folder across the heavy oak desk. It's thick—these guys don't mess around about their security.

I open the folder and on the top is a full-sized portrait of Princess Sarah. Taken at a state dinner earlier this year, she's dressed in gold from head to toe in a form-fitting strapless gown that hugs her every curve. I swallow hard and set the folder in my lap to hide my boner.

With sun-kissed tan skin, long waves of dark brown hair, and a pout on her lips that could tempt a saint, the princess might be the most gorgeous woman I've ever seen.

And the stuffiest.

There's something about her perfectly coiffed hair and flawless make-up that makes me want to mess it up a little. A bruising kiss to smear her lipstick. A hand down her top to cup her breasts. Another hand tangled in her hair, letting loose locks fall over her shoulders.

My cock jerks to life in my pants.

I flip the photo over to read a report on the recent threat level. Fury slices through me, and I have an overwhelming urge to punch someone. Anyone.

I glance up to meet Georgio's equally hard stare. "That's a lot of new threats against the princess."

"Rhodon is an old, traditional kingdom. No woman has sat on the throne in two-hundred years."

"And a lot of people aren't too happy about that." Great. Nothing like some backward thinking people to complicate progress. Not to mention threaten the life of a woman so beautiful, her face has filled my dreams the past few nights.

"That's why you're here." Georgio folds his hands on the desk. "Though some of us think the princess should be informed about the severity of these threats, the king has ordered us to keep them confidential."

"Why?" Doesn't a woman have a right to know when her life is in danger?

"The king doesn't want her to worry. Thinks she has enough on her plate."

It's not much of an excuse. "But wouldn't it make things easier if she knew?"

"It's your job to keep her safe."

The way he says it leaves no room for discussion or debate. Seeing that I'll let the matter rest—for now at least—Georgio rises. "Let's go meet her."

I follow him out of the wood-paneled office and into a long corridor. With vaulted ceilings and paintings in gold frames lining the walls, this place is every inch a palace. It's like I've stepped into one of those princess movies my sister used to watch on repeat when we were kids.

We make a few more turns, go up one staircase and down another before we come to stand outside a pair of double doors. A footman bows his head to Georgio and slips inside. I shove my hands in my pockets and glance around, noting the ornate vase on an equally ancient end table. There are a lot of breakables in this place. I'm almost afraid to move for fear of knocking something over. The footman returns a moment later and pulls open the door.

Georgio leads the way into the room. This one is decorated with softer colors and fabrics, vases overflowing with flowers that give the room a fragrant scent.

And there, seated on a high-backed antique sofa is the most stunning woman I've ever seen.

"Your highness, may I present Ryan Timmons. Your new guard."

She rises to her feet. Dressed more casually in a flowy top and some of those cropped pants my sister says are trendy, she's every bit as gorgeous as her picture.

Maybe even more so. My cock swells, and I lower the folder so it won't give me away. Georgio stares at me, then jerks his head. Oh, shit. Bending at the waist, I bow and murmur, "Ma'am."

Straightening, I look up and straight into her dark brown

eyes. She might as well reach out and grab my dick. *Down boy.*

Slowly, she raises her hand and holds it out to me. Though I'd rather push her up against a wall and make her mine, I take the offered hand and shake. Warm, soft skin sends heat radiating through me. I release her hand and take a step back.

"If you will leave us," she says, dismissing Georgio and the footman. Now we're alone. Too alone.

"I looked over your resume." She arches an eyebrow. "Quite impressive. I am afraid you will be rather bored following me to breakfast meetings and ballets."

"It will be my pleasure." More of one than she will ever know.

"Let us cut to the chase. I do not require your services."

"Your father thinks otherwise."

"Yes, well, I still—"

I raise my hand to cut her off and her eyes widen. Shit. She's probably never been interrupted in her life. It's a good thing her father is my boss and not her. Otherwise, I'd be packing my bags already.

"With all due respect," I say, keeping my tone gentle and contrite. "It's my job to keep you alive. I'll be sticking to your side like glue until your father says otherwise."

Her eyes cool and, for some reason, her glare is even more intoxicating than those pouty lips. "We will have to see about that."

THREE

SARAH

The man is insufferable. It hasn't even been a full day since Ryan stormed into our castle—and my life. I am barely allowed to set foot outside my bedroom without having him following close behind. He even stands outside the powder room door when I tend to more delicate matters.

And, let me tell you, it is beyond difficult to tend to nature's call when a man who looks like he stepped out of a Hollywood action movie is standing within earshot. Him with his cropped, dirty blond hair, stubble-covered jaw, and a pair of hazel eyes so piercing, I might need a doctor to check my heart.

I understand it is his job to hover. But sometimes a woman needs a moment to herself.

Especially when her imagination keeps wandering into dangerous territory. Like what it would be like to be swept up into those strong arms of his. What it would feel like to tear the tie from his neck and rip open the buttons on his shirt so I can splay my fingers over his undoubtedly ripped abs and chest.

I suck in a breath and fan myself with the printout of services someone on the hospital staff handed me when we arrived for our visit.

"Are you okay, ma'am?" Ryan asks in a low voice.

"I am fine." As long as I do not let my imagination run wild. "I am not as delicate as people might think."

His lips twitch, but he says nothing, turning his attention back to scanning the room.

Today I am here to cut another ribbon. Yesterday afternoon was a new statue honoring veterans. Today is for a new trauma ward at the hospital. While I passionately care about both organizations, I am less enthused about standing up in front of crowds taking credit for other people's work.

A doctor finishes his remarks with surprising flourish and steps aside. This is my cue. Plastering on a bright smile, I suck in a breath and step toward the microphone.

"On behalf of my father, the King, and my family, I am deeply honored to be here with you to commemorate this momentous occasion. It is our sincere hope that these new facilities will provide all who reside here with the best possible care and our doctors with the equipment necessary to save lives." I break from my reading to glance at the courteous, but unsmiling, audience. "Thank you to everyone who made this possible and to everyone who works every day to keep the people of Rhodon healthy and safe."

I step back, and there's a polite buzz of applause. Someone hands the doctor and I each a pair of scissors. We pause for the cameras—my cheeks aching. When we get the nod, we cut and the ribbon falls aside to cheers.

With my part done, I return to my spot in the background. Beside me, Ryan stoically stares around the now more animated room.

"Nice speech."

I start at his remark. "It was pretty standard."

"There's nothing standard about you."

His face remains impassive, but his words are warm, like a caress down my spine. Is it my imagination running wild again, or is the sexy bodyguard with a jaw that could cut diamonds flirting with me?

My heart flutters.

Before I can issue a witty or flirty response of my own, Ryan touches his ear and nods. "We're good to go."

Placing a hand on the small of my back, he ushers me through the crowd. While I may not like his pushiness, I rather enjoy the feel of his warm, hard hand on my back. If only it was touching my bare skin. My cheeks flush hot red.

He glances down at me again and frowns. "Are you sure you're okay?"

"I am quite well."

I increase my stride and am nearly out the door when someone calls out, "Your highness."

I turn to find a reporter I recognize as a royal correspondent from the country's largest publication. Though I would like nothing more than to slip out the door without comment, my father's words about honor and duty come to mind.

The perma-smile back in place, I step away from the door, Ryan so close behind me, we almost touch. The man oozes sexuality and masculinity. I can practically taste it.

"Highness, any comment on those who say you're not equipped to run our country."

My smile almost falters, but I keep my spine straight. "When the time comes, I will serve our country to the best of my ability."

"But wouldn't it make more sense to step aside and let your brother do the job?"

I nearly say yes, but I feel Ryan's hand cup my arm.

"I hate to interrupt, but we have to go."

Relief floods through me. The journalist wilts under Ryan's sharp stare.

A moment later, I am outside, and before I can blink, I am in the back of my car. I let out a breath I did not realize I was holding.

"Thank you for that," I say.

Ryan meets my gaze in the rearview mirror. "I'm here to serve and protect."

I am not sure rescuing me from an impertinent reporter falls under the category of his job description, but I am grateful all the same.

RYAN

There are far too many people streaming into the opera house for my liking. Apparently, *The Barber of Seville* is the hottest ticket in town this evening. Who knew?

It's tempting to encourage Sarah—or rather, the princess —to stay in with a book or movie tonight. But her father made it damn clear she needs to be seen in full battle wear tonight. I'm not sure how dressing up in an overpriced ball gown and a tiara proves strength to the public. But I'm not here to question the monarchy. I'm here to keep the princess safe.

That task has been a bit easier since the run-in at the hospital this morning. My intervention with the journalist seems to have created a truce of sorts between us.

I turn from my spot in the passenger seat to see how she's holding up. The flashes from the camera flicker on her face and glitter in the diamond tiara nestled in her hair. She has it pulled up like it was in the photo, exposing her long neck. I clench my fists to keep from giving in to the urge to reach back and run a finger over her bare shoulder.

Glancing out the window at the waiting crowd, I hope tonight's audience is gentle.

"Ready, ma'am?"

Her dark gaze flitters to meet mine. There's an edge of fear in her eyes. I'm filled with the urge to reach out and pull her into my arms.

Taking a deep breath through her nose, she nods. "Ready as ever."

Throwing open my door, I step around the car alerting the guard standing in the entryway that we're going in.

As I reach her door, I give another look around. There aren't any figures on rooftops or in windows. Nothing turned up in the sweep ten minutes ago. Still, I'll feel better once she's in the royal box.

Pulling open her door, I offer my hand. Placing her gloved hand in mine, she sets one high-heeled foot out the door. As she rises to her feet, a chorus of boos begin.

Sarah's grip tightens, and she freezes.

"Are they booing me?" she asks in a low voice.

The crestfallen expression on her face tugs at my heart.

"Quick. Let's get inside."

With her hand clasped in mine, I keep her close as we push through the crowd. One angry man lunges out from her. She gasps and I throw a protective arm over her shoulder, keeping her out of range.

We pick up our pace and are in a moment later. I barely pay attention to the famed marble floors or ornate architecture as we wordlessly move up the stairs. Neither of us speaks as we race to the royal box.

Once she's seated, I kneel in front of her. She's gone pale, and the light seems to have left her eyes. Her pain gnaws at my gut.

"Can I get you something? Maybe some water?"

She shakes her head.

"I am not ready for this."

"The opera?"

"Being queen. I'm never going to be ready for this."

A single tear slips down her cheek. It's all I can do not to fold her into my arms.

"You will be when the time comes." I squeeze her hand. "I have no doubt."

Another tear falls, along with my heart. "Did you hear them out there? They hate me."

"No one hates you."

She gives an indelicate snort. I smile as some of the fire rekindles in her eyes.

"They do not seem to particularly care for me." Her pout is back. "I was fine when I was their partying princess. Like a silly pet or something. But now . . . they do not want me. What if they never give me a chance?"

I wish I could give her specifics about how to win over her country and the people in it. But maybe my tips aren't important right now. Maybe she just needs a good old-fashioned pep talk.

I tip her chin up with my finger. "Right now there are some people who may think they don't want you as your queen. But they need you."

"They don't need me."

"They do." My thumb runs over her smooth skin. "They don't know what you're capable of doing. They don't know what's in your heart."

"And you do?"

I lift a shoulder. "I know it's only been a couple of days, but I saw how much compassion you had when you visited the patients at the hospital. I know you stayed up half the night reading textbooks and documents."

I hesitate a moment and even though I may live to regret it, I raise her hand to my lips and give it a brief kiss. "You will make them see how lucky they are to have you. In the meantime, I'm here."

Because while this may have been another paycheck a few days ago, now I know I can't leave Sarah's side until I know she's good and safe.

FOUR

SARAH

I have a plan. It came to me last night while Figaro sang his signature song made famous by Bugs Bunny and Elmer Fudd. All I have to do is give a quick speech at this economic development breakfast and lose my security detail.

Which, I admit, will not be easy. Not with the way Ryan never takes his eyes off me for longer than a quick scan of the room. Even now, as I wrap up my speech about the importance of supporting the local industry, I can feel his eyes on me.

I fight a twinge of guilt at what I am about to do. But I can't afford to get caught up in emotions. Especially not where Ryan is concerned.

As the business leaders join me in a mimosa toast, I take only a taste for courage before setting the glass aside.

While everyone returns to their plates of pastries and fruit, I move toward the hallway leading to the back. I have barely taken two steps when Ryan grabs my arm.

"Your car is waiting on the other side."

"I know. But I left my purse in the powder room."

His eyes narrow, but he gives a short nod.

A wave of relief rushes over me, but I keep my face neutral. I have come too far to go back now. In the powder room, I grab my bag and lock the door. I make quick work of stripping out of my dress and into a pair of jeans and a T-shirt. Scrubbing the makeup from my face, I pull my hair back into a tight bun. With a cropped blonde wig and a pair of oversized sunglasses to finish my look, I step back to study my disguise in the mirror.

I blink in disbelief. I hardly recognize the woman staring back at me. That bodes well for my ability to slip away undetected. I tuck cash into my back pocket and stuff my dress into the oversized bag. I hide it under the sink, hoping it will take at least a few minutes for Ryan to bust open the door and discover I have gone incognito.

My heart races in my ears as I push a chair under the window. Doing my best to be quiet, I push the window open. Sucking in a breath, I pull myself up and over the ledge. It is a short drop to the ground outside.

I walk briskly to the dock just behind the restaurant. Pulling out the fake ID I used to use in college with my girlfriends, the dock agent shows me to the boat I rented first thing this morning.

Excitement bubbles inside of me as I cast off and turn on the boat's engine. I cannot believe it worked. Just as planned, I made it from the podium to the water in just five minutes. If my calculations are correct, Ryan is only now realizing I am no longer inside. Pushing the throttle, I pull away from the dock.

Thud.

My heart leaps into my throat. I turn to find my body-guard standing on the back of the boat. His chest rising up and down, his hazel eyes narrow.

"Where do you think you're going?"

RYAN

When she doesn't immediately answer my question, I repeat it with more heat. "Where do you think you're going?"

I wait for her to fumble out an excuse or an apology. I'm not prepared for her to throw her head back and laugh.

My patience is gone, my hands ball into fists at my side. I practically roar, "What the fuck are you doing?"

She falls silent and her eyes widen.

"No one besides my brothers has ever used that word around me."

I'm not going to let her guilt me into forgetting that we're currently pushing farther and farther away from the shore.

If I hadn't heard the bathroom window creak open, I might have missed her. As it was, I rounded the building in time to watch her saunter down to the dock. If she'd been a little quieter, she could be halfway to God knows where before I figured it out.

I fight a fresh wave of fury. I run my fingers through my hair. "Princess, I need you to level with me. What's going on here?"

Her shoulders slump. "Last night, at the opera, I realized I need one day. Just one day to be no one before I spend the rest of my life serving the people of my country. Whether or not they hate me."

A tear slips down her cheeks, and my resistance slips.

"You realize what's going to happen when your father finds out?"

"I can tell him I knocked you out. Kidnapped you."

I chuckle at that. "Don't you think that would look worse for me?"

She watches me carefully, her expression hopeful. "You won't make me go back?"

"I won't make you go back." I sigh. "Where are we headed?"

A bright smile explodes across her face a second before she throws her arms around me. My hands come up instinctively, molding to her curves. My body comes alive at her touch. Including my cock, which is aching to be inside of her.

I shake the thought from my head.

"Barcelona is only a couple hours away by boat," she says.

"I'll need to let someone know you're okay."

She nods and pulls away. "But then no more cell phones."

"No more cell phones." I used to be a hard-nosed warrior no one could push around. Now she's turned me into putty. "Princess, this better be worth it."

"It will be." She grins again. "I need one more favor."

"You don't want my kidney do you?" Or maybe my heart.

"Do you think that for today I could just be Sarah and you can just be Ryan?"

Her words do something to my heart. "With pleasure."

Now that I am committed to what is likely treason, I type in a quick message to Georgio and turn off my phone.

Though it's still early, the sun is already beating down on us here in the open water. I shrug out of my suit jacket and toss aside my tie. I'm rolling up my sleeves when I catch Sarah staring at me. If I'm not mistaken, her gaze is every bit as hungry as mine.

Maybe a day alone with her isn't such a good idea. It will take every ounce of my willpower to keep my hands off of her.

But even as I vow to do just that, my body and heart scream to make her mine.

FIVE

SARAH

Bursting with laughter, Ryan and I stumble into a studio flat near Las Rambla.

"I cannot believe you 'know a guy' with an empty apartment." I shake my head. "Just like you knew a guy who could get us tickets to the football match."

"When you spend the better part of a decade in the military, you get to know a lot of people." Ryan grins, and I swear the air around us turns up a degree or two. "I can't believe you won a beer-drinking contest. And that you picked a fight at the match."

"That woman was being impossibly rude. How low do you have to stoop to steal a free T-shirt from a small child?"

"Luckily, you were there to slay the dragon and get it back for him. With a little more training, you could put me out of a job."

I wave off the remark, though my heart bursts at his compliment.

It has been an incredible day. We arrived in Barcelona just after noon. After grabbing a bite to eat at a cafe and strolling through the markets, we started up to Parc Güell. Then Ryan found a payphone and made a call. An hour later we were sneaking into the FC Barcelona game.

We finished our evening by sharing a bottle of wine and tapas at another restaurant. Ryan told me about growing up in a small town in eastern Washington state. I told him about the years I spent at university in England and the taste of anonymity that came with them. He tells me about following his father into the military. I tell him about being the only daughter in a family of boys. He tells me about his mom's peach pie. I tell him about my favorite spot in the palace gardens.

There are people I have known a lifetime who know me less than this man. No one makes me feel more at peace.

There is only one thing I want—one thing I need at this moment. He is standing in front of me with a glass of water.

I take the glass from his hand and set it aside. He eyes me curiously, but I don't give him a chance to speak. I throw my arms around his neck and pull his mouth to mine. He jolts in surprise. For a moment I worry he will push me away. But his arms come up and wrap around me. Moving up and down my back, over every curve of my body.

My lips part and our tongues meet. I moan as one of his hands lowers, grabbing my derrière, pulling me close enough to feel his hard length against my belly. My fingers dive into his cropped hair, and I know this will not be enough.

I want—need—him all.

I lower my hands to the waist of his pants. I palm him through the fabric as I reach for the button.

He jerks back. "Sarah . . . Princess . . . Sarah. We can't—"

"You said that for today we could be Ryan and Sarah."

He releases a breath and nods. "I did say that."

"What would Ryan do to Sarah right now?"

His eyes lift to mine. "He'd take her to bed and fuck her until neither of them could think straight."

His words send a fresh thrill through my body. "Then let's be Ryan and Sarah."

Fortunately, I do not have to tell him twice. He reaches for me, pulling me toward the bed. When he tries to tug my shirt up, I bat his hand away.

He gapes at me in surprise. I shake my head and press a finger to his lips. "There is something Sarah is eager to do first."

I take advantage of his confusion and push him toward the bed. I reach for the button on his pants again as I sink to my knees.

His eyes widen before his eyelids lower in a sultry, sexy way. "I didn't think princesses kneeled to anyone."

"In the bedroom, all protocol goes out the window."

I unzip his pants and reach into his boxer briefs, releasing his hard length. My stomach flutters and my mouth waters in anticipation. I run my hand up and down his shaft and he groans.

"Careful there, baby. Or this will be over before it starts."

"Sounds like a challenge."

He kicks off his shoes, and I pull his pants and boxers to the ground. My mouth covers him. My tongue runs over the tip, his salty taste fills my senses. I lower my head, taking more of him in my mouth as my hand moves up and down him.

He groans, digging his fingers in my hair, urging me on. His enthusiasm only makes me hungrier. My free hand grabs onto his backside, pulling him deeper inside of me. My tongue, my lips, my fingers urge him on.

"Oh, God, baby. You feel so good." He groans again. "I can't wait to taste you next."

The image of his head between my thighs instantly soaks my panties. I hum with anticipation, even as I taste his.

My head bobs up and down, silently begging him to give me what I want. To give me all of him. He tenses below my fingertips and with my name—only my name—on my lips, he comes hard, shooting his seed into my mouth.

I lean back on my heels and glance up at him. His eyes are clenched shut, his jaw is slack as he takes deep breaths. Catching my stare, he pulls me to my feet, bringing my lips to his again. His hand slips down to the waist of my jeans and under the band. His mouth moves from mine, trailing kisses along my cheek and down my neck. Fresh waves of arousal pulse through me.

"That was incredible," he murmurs near my ear. "Now it's my turn."

Tugging off my shirt, he gently pushes me to the bed so my legs hang over the edge. I lean up as he tugs my jeans and panties down my hips. He kisses where his fingers have been.

"I love your body." He takes a playful nip at my hip. "It's so soft. So sweet." Then his gaze meets mine, and a wicked smile crosses his lips. "Better grab a hold of something, sweetheart."

RYAN

I slide one hand around to Sarah's sweet, round ass, while my finger slips through the fold to find her. My tongue traces the inside of her thigh. She shivers and tangles her fingers into my hair.

I rub my cheek against her inner thigh as my thumb

traces her clit. Her thighs press against my ears. I chuckle as I slip my tongue up to take my first taste of her. Her gasp mingles with my moan. She's even sweeter than I imagined.

My tongue laps her up. I feast on her like she's Thanksgiving dinner. I slide one finger inside of her. Then another. She's so tight. She bucks up against me, crying out. My other hand moves up and over her hip. I press down on her belly, tracing my thumb through her neatly cut bush, holding her in place.

"Ryan." Her grip on my hair tightens. "Oh, Ryan. Yes. Yes."

Her cries turn into screams as I feel her tremble against my mouth and hand. I stay with her as the orgasm ripples through her body.

As she lies there on the bed drawing in deep breaths, my hand traces up her curves. I join her on the bed, my mouth moving where my hands have been. My hands cup her breasts through the lace of her bra. My dick aches again with need. God, she's beautiful. And her breasts—so full, so soft—feel even better than I imagined.

Watching her come, and the taste of her on my lips has me hard again.

I slip the straps of her bra over her shoulder and tug one breast free. My mouth comes over the nipple while my fingers prod and pinch the other. Her breathing quickens again, and she moves against me.

"Oh, Ryan."

When I can feel her reaching another peak, she grabs at me. She pulls me up so her tongue can dual with mine. I like that she's a woman who knows what she wants and takes it. She may be all prim and proper at ribbon cuttings and operas. But in a soccer match and bed, she is wild and untamed.

Her lips tear from mine. "I need you inside of me."

I bet I need to be inside of her more.

While I'd love nothing more than to ride her bare right now, I reach for my wallet and remove a condom. Though we've crossed the line, I can never forget who she is and who I am. I'd love to fill her with my seed, but I know her position as the future queen comes with expectations and obligations.

Having the child of an American nobody isn't on a future queen's to-do list.

Rolling the condom on over my hard length, I move on to my back and pull her on top of me. Her thighs on either side of my hips, she sinks back slowly. My fingers lace with hers. I hiss through clenched teeth as she takes me inch by inch.

Sweet, Jesus. I'm in heaven again. She leans back until her ass is flush with my hips. She moves forward once, twice. Teasing me, teasing her. I savor the play for as long as I can. Until I can't take another second.

I release her hands and grab her hips, thrusting up to meet her move for move as I urge her to move faster, harder. She throws her head back. One hand moves up her belly to cover her breast. The other lowers to where our bodies are joined. Watching her touch herself, pleasure herself nearly takes me over the edge.

But I need her to come first.

"Come on baby. Come for me."

And almost on cue, she does. Her muscles grip my cock, pulling my pleasure into hers and pushing hers into mine. I empty myself into the condom as she shouts my name once more.

When the last wave of pleasure has run through us both, she collapses on top of me. Our chests rise up and down. Our hearts pound against each other.

I press my lips to her temple and trace my fingers over her back. There will never be another woman for me. Even as my head screams that it's impossible, my thundering heart tells it to shut up. Whether or not she kicks me to the curb or her father throws me into a dungeon, she has my heart. I am hers now and forever, come what may. And she is mine.

SIX

SARAH

We are back on the boat before the sun rises over the hills. Even though I am settled in my love's lap as he steers us toward land, my spirits sink. My heart splinters with every mile we move closer to Rhodon. I sincerely doubt anything awaiting me there can measure up to the perfection of yesterday—to being simply Sarah and Ryan.

Seemingly sensing my train of thoughts, Ryan lifts a hand to my shoulder and massages. I look up and into his serious eyes.

"Do we have to go back?"

His lips curve into a sad smile. "I'm pretty sure your dad will have my head on a stake as it is. If I don't get you back by lunch, he'll probably have my balls on spikes, too."

I cannot help but giggle at that, but I sober again quickly.

"I meant do we have to go back to the way we were before yesterday?" Unable to look at him, I face forward, where Rhodon grows closer and closer. "I know we said yesterday was a free pass, but . . . "

How do I tell him? How do I tell this man I want more when I do not know how there can ever be more?

Ryan's hand slips down my arm, leaving goosebumps in its wake and slides around my stomach. "Your father will probably fire me. But I'm not going anywhere. Ever."

I raise my hands to cover his arm, hugging him close to me. I know this is fast. I know there are a million reasons why my father—and everyone—will say we cannot be together. But when I am with this man, everything feels possible.

Even ruling the country.

We reach land within the hour. Pulling the boat to the marina, Ryan swears under his breath. I follow his gaze and mutter a few choice words of my own. There on the dock is a full contingent of the palace guard with the senior guard himself standing with his arms crossed.

"Looks like we have a welcome party."

I glance up at Ryan. "Maybe we should become pirates."

"I think it's a little late for piracy, Princess."

We have barely turned off the engine when guards surround the boat. Ryan jumps onto the deck first, offering a hand to me. He pulls me up and against him for a moment.

"We will figure this out," he whispers, pressing a kiss below my ear. "I'm not going anywhere."

He releases me then and turns toward Georgio. The two men exchange a look I cannot quite decipher before the senior guard turns his stare to me.

"Princess, I think you should come with me."

Georgio reaches for my arm, but Ryan pulls me back against his chest. "You might be my boss for a few more minutes, but no one touches the princess on my watch."

I brace myself for Georgio's wrath—ready to intervene on

Ryan's behalf. Only, instead of ordering his minions to haul Ryan away, I swear the guy is fighting a smile. I cannot remember ever seeing my father's head of security express even a hint of humor.

Satisfied neither of us will be dragged anywhere without our say, I glance up at Ryan and catch the frown on his face.

"Two o'clock," he says. "By the popcorn vendor."

Georgio swivels. I've barely shifted my gaze when someone shouts. Ryan wraps himself around me and pulls me to the ground a second before I hear it. The unmistakable crack of a gunshot.

I clench my eyes shut, my hands pressed to the wood-planked ground. Ryan's arms squeeze me tighter, and he jerks. My heart thunders in my chest, in my ears, in my knees. It beat, beat, beats through me, my blood running cold.

In the distance, more shouts and movement whirl around us like a dream or nightmare.

"You okay?" Ryan whispers in my ear.

I manage a short nod.

"Good." He presses a kiss against my hair. "Just take a few deep breaths for me."

His thumb moves over my belly, soothing me into doing what he's ordered. It works. After a few deep breaths in and out, my heart steadies and the world comes into focus.

I open my eyes in time to see a shadow kneel in front of us. Based on the polished shoes and black slacks, it's one of the palace guards.

"We have someone down here," he calls out. "We need a medic."

I shake my head at the over-the-top response.

"I am fine," I insist.

"That's good, baby," Ryan says.

It takes me a moment to recognize the tension in it.

Before I can ask what's wrong, someone pries Ryan away from me and onto his back. Another guard offers me a hand, but I ignore it. I push myself up onto my knees and turn.

Georgio hovers over Ryan, a red handkerchief pressed to his arm. No. Not a red handkerchief. A white handkerchief covered in blood.

Ryan has been shot.

"No!" I scramble to his other side, gripped by a terror I have never known. I barely reach him when I am pulled away by another faceless guard. I shove and push to no avail. "Let me go!"

"It's not safe for you here, ma'am. We don't know if the area is secured."

"But Ryan." I wriggle again, struggling for breath. "I need to be with him."

"He's in good hands."

I would rather see to his care myself, but no amount of flailing and clawing works. I am in the back of a black car, which skids away before the guard loosens his hold.

I press my face against the window, but all I see is a crowd of observers. The siren of first responders wails in the distance, but we disappear into a tunnel before it arrives.

SEVEN

RYAN

The shooting pain in my arm jerks me awake. I'm clutching at it before I open my eyes. There's a white bandage wrapped around it. And I'm wearing a damned paper dress.

The dock. The gunfire.

Sarah.

I bolt up, but a hand pushes me back down.

"Careful there, young man. You'll pull out your IV and tear your stitches."

I turn toward the voice and find Georgio. Of course. The king must have sent him here to fire me. A guy can be laid up from taking a bullet, but when he's sleeping with the future queen, there's no time to waste.

"Is Sarah—the princess—is she okay?"

Georgio's stern expression softens. "Not even a scratch. The man who fired the weapon is in police custody. He appears to have acted alone."

Relief floods through me. She's okay. Not even a scratch.

"Just how much trouble am I?"

He lifts a shoulder. "You bled like crazy, but it's just a flesh wound."

A flesh wound that hurts like hell. I made it through four tours in war zones with a few scrapes and bruises. But a few days on the job watching a reluctant princess, and I'm laid up. How's that for a kick in the pants?

"You didn't answer me before. How much trouble am I?" I lift my arm, wincing at the pain as I let it drop back to my side. "Because I'll tell you this. The king can fire me. He can try to kick me out of the country. But I'm not going anywhere until Sarah says otherwise."

"I don't know." Georgio pulls a face. "The king can be a stubborn man."

"He hasn't met me." I'll give him hell, king or not.

"No. He hasn't." A slow grin spreads across Georgio's face. "But I have. And I'll tell you this. As far as I'm concerned, you're not going anywhere."

I arch an eyebrow. "You'd defy the king?"

"Within reason." He chuckles at that. "And while I have no doubt you have a long, difficult road ahead of you, I'd say you proved something today."

"What, that I can take a bullet?"

"That you'd take one for the woman you love." Georgio pats me on the shoulder. "As a father myself, I can't tell you of anything else I'd like better in a future son-in-law."

SARAH

Father wastes no time calling me to the throne room for a tongue-lashing. He is waiting for me the moment I set foot in the palace.

"Do you have any idea of what could have happened to you?"

"Happened to me?" I wipe the tears that will not stop falling from my face with the back of my hand. "How about what happened to Ryan?"

The memory of him lying on the ground, blood pouring from his arm, lances my heart. Another sob wracks my body.

Father frowns. "You mean the bodyguard who should have kept you from leaving in the first place?"

"He was doing his job."

"His job was to keep you here." He pulls back his shoulders like he is preparing himself to launch into a full speech.

But I am not in the mood for speeches. Not when I have no idea of whether or not Ryan is okay.

"Before you say anything else, before you scream about duty and honor, please." A fresh tear slips down my cheek. "How is he?"

Father's frown stays firmly in place, but he sighs. "Georgio says he needs a few stitches. They want to keep him overnight, but he'll be free to go in the morning."

"Oh thank God." I wrap my arms around myself and fall to the ground in relief. "Thank God."

"What are you doing?"

"Praying." I clench my eyes shut.

Thank you, God, for saving Ryan. Thank you, God, for bringing him into my life.

When my eyes open again, I catch the interest in my father's eyes. For the first time since I walked in the door, he does not look angry or upset. Just . . . interested.

I release a shaky breath. "I think you should know something."

He says nothing, but nods for me to continue.

"I have found the man I intend to marry."

His eyes widen. "Surely you do not mean—"

"I do. I am in love with Ryan." I push myself up to my feet so I can stare my father in the eye as I tell him what is in my heart. "Ever since we learned about the falsified paperwork, I have been terrified. I did not know how I could ever hope to be queen. But Ryan makes me stronger. Like I can—and should—be queen."

Father's jaw tightens. "Georgio speaks highly of him. And I have read his record. But with all of the distrust running rampant, surely you cannot plan to make a life with a common American."

"Mother did not have a title." I lift my chin. "And before you say that is different, or that it is not allowed, rest assured that I have read our country's constitution and rules from beginning to end. I know as queen I can choose my husband."

"But you are not the queen."

"Not yet. But I will wait until I am to marry Ryan if you do not give your blessing and permission sooner. I'll wait, even if it means I am an old woman."

Hesitating a moment, I take my father's hand. "But, Father . . . Dad. You know the weight of wearing the crown. Surely you can appreciate what it means to have someone at your side who makes you the best version of yourself to serve the country."

My father swallows. "Then I suppose there is only one thing left to do." He turns his hand over to take mine. "I had better go meet my future son-in-law."

EIGHT

RYAN

I'll be damned if I'm staying here overnight. I struggle to pull on a T-shirt when there's a knock at my hospital room door. Georgio enters.

"You have a visitor."

I tug the shirt down so I can glare at him. "Do I look like I'm fit for company?"

"You'll want to see this visitor." He smirks. "But you'll probably want to be dressed."

Before I can ask what he means, two more men in dark suits enter the room followed by a man I recognize from the money in my wallet. The king.

Pulling the shirt on over one shoulder, and down to cover half my chest, I rise to my feet and bow. "Your royal highness."

He nods and the three other men leave the room. Georgio gives me a parting wink on his way out. I'm going to kick his ass just as soon as I'm out of here.

The king spares the room a quick look before taking a seat next to the bed. He gestures for me to sit. Following my soldier's training, I do as ordered.

He clears his throat. "It has come to my attention that you have stolen the most important treasure in my kingdom."

I shake my head. "Your majesty, I . . . "

He holds up a hand. "My daughter, it would seem, has decided you are the only man for her."

His words clutch at my heart. I feel like I could burst with the joy of it. "Did she say that?"

"I have just one question for you: What do you plan to do about that?"

Dozens of visions fill my mind. Of pledging my love and life to her in a church surrounded by our friends and family—and undoubtedly more than a thousand other guests. Of watching our children play in the gardens at the palace. Of growing old and gray together. Of helping each other through the ups and downs of whatever life throws our way.

"I plan to be at her side every step of the way from this day forward."

"And you understand what that means?" The king's eyes narrow. "My daughter is not just a common woman."

"There's nothing common about your daughter, Sir. With or without a crown."

The king studies me silently, then rises to his feet. I follow. He holds out a hand. I stare at it a moment before I realize he wants me to shake it.

As I do, he leans in. "You saved her life. I leave you to help her live it to the fullest."

He leaves me there staring after him. I'm pretty sure the king just gave me his blessing. I'd better go find his daughter and make her mine.

I'm reaching for my coat when there's another rap at the

door. This time, I glance up to find the most beautiful and enchanting woman standing there. I raise a hand in greeting but wince at the strain on my stitches. She rushes forward, tears in her eyes. She opens her mouth to speak. But then she's in my arms. My lips are on hers. And all is right in the world.

When we pull apart, she gives a shaky breath. "I am so sorry this happened. I hope you will forgive me."

"There's nothing to forgive."

"You saved my life." Her voice breaks. "I will never be able to repay you for that."

"You already have." I lift one of her hands to my lips. "I know you said you didn't need a bodyguard hanging around. But you're not getting rid of me now. I'd give my life for you."

She shakes her head. "No. Please. You cannot say that."

"You might not like it, but it's the truth. I'd die for you, Sarah. Not because it's my job or because you'll one day be the queen." I rest my forehead against hers. "But I love you. And I give everything—my heart, my life—to what I love."

She murmurs my name and wraps her arms around me. "I love you too. And I offer you my heart and my life if you will take them."

"With pleasure."

Then my lips find hers again, and there is no need to say anything more.

EPILOGUE

SARAH

six months later

Stepping through the corridor, I pause at a heavy oak door. I cast a glance over my shoulder to make sure I am alone. Once I am positive no footsteps or shadows are lurking, I kick off my high-heel shoes and pull two pins from the hair piled on top of my head. Bending them the way I was shown, I chew on my bottom lip as I wiggle and push the pins in the lock.

Click

I'm in. Grinning, I slowly turn the door handle and inch it open so it will not creek. On my tiptoes, I creep inside. I am barely in the room when the door slams behind me and a hand slips over my mouth to stifle a scream.

I am pulled against a solid, muscular chest and an arm slips around my waist. My heart pounds as my chest rises up and down.

"You could have knocked," Ryan whispers in my ear.

I push his hand away from my mouth. "What would be the fun in that?"

"You're gonna make me regret showing that little party trick, aren't you?"

"As often as I can. You know I like to keep you on your toes."

"I'm counting on it."

Chuckling, he presses a kiss to the side of my head. Then he spins me around in his arms to grin down at me. My heart flutters. In just ten more hours, this strong, handsome man will be my husband. And I will be his wife. Ryan and Sarah Timmons. Nevermind the fancy titles that will come.

He strokes my back. "Having trouble sleeping?"

I nod.

"Not having any regrets, I hope?"

"Never." I lean up on my toes to kiss his chin. "You are stuck with me forever, Your Grace."

"I like the sounds of that." Closing his eyes, he rests his forehead against mine and sighs. "Unless your father has a change of heart."

"Doubtful. Now that you are the Duke of Orkhis, you are basically royal yourself." I grin. "Plus he would lose the deposit on the champagne. And we've spent a small fortune on the cake."

"We picked out some pretty damn good champagne and cake. Especially with that celebrity baker you flew in just for me." He kisses my nose. "It would be a shame to miss them."

"Yes, well, about that." I lean back in his arms so I can look up at him. "I am afraid my champagne drinking days are behind me."

He arches an eyebrow.

"At least for now." Unable to contain a grin, I place one of his hands on my belly. "I'm told a sip or two won't hurt the baby, but—"

His mouth falls open. "You're pregnant."

I nod. "I know it is ahead of schedule, but—"

He captures my lips in a searing kiss. As love pours from him into me, I am not worried about whether or not this is too soon or how we will balance a family with our royal responsibilities. Whatever happens, we have each other. Now and always.

When we part, Ryan's face breaks into a smile.

"I love you so much." He cups my cheek. "Do you have any idea how rich you've made my life?"

He does not give me a chance to answer, because his lips are on mine again. I will just have to tell him later that I know exactly what he means. Birth order may have made me the future queen of Rhodon. But fate blessed me by bringing this man into my life. That is worth more than all the palaces and jewels in the world.

ALEX

RIDICULOUSLY ROYAL #2

Copyright © 2020 by Kate Tilney

This is a work of fiction. Names, characters, places, and incidents are either the product of the author's imagination or are used fictitiously, and any resemblance to actual persons, living or dead, events, or locales is entirely coincidental.

All Rights Reserved. No part of this book may be reproduced or transmitted in any form or by any means, electronic or mechanical, including photocopying, recording, or by any information storage and retrieval system, without permission in writing from the author.

Cover Photos by

nemetse/ depositphotos

feedough/ depositphotos

ONE

ALEX

I never thought anything could be more intense than the heat of battle. I suppose, in a way, attending the wedding of the crowned princess of Rhodon is not so different from a combat zone. Especially because the bride-to-be is my sister and my father—the king—has called all hands on deck.

Talk about the heat of battle.

With so many of the royal families and dignitaries from around the world staying in the palace this week, it is rather like the close quarters we have in a barracks.

And like in the military, we all have our responsibilities and duties. When I am in the field, I am a helicopter pilot transporting soldiers and equipment as necessary. While I am still awaiting all my marching orders for the wedding, I'm fairly confident mine will involve transport of some sort. Especially if my mother's Aunt Muriel has any champagne before the ceremony. The last time that happened, she ended up hitting on the priest before passing out beside the altar.

Even though my sister has been pretty lax about all things wedding, I imagine she would rather avoid having a drunk, amorous relative upstaging her nuptials.

Then again, she may not notice. These days she only has eyes for her fiancé.

At least she's marrying a normal guy. Ryan, the newly dubbed Duke of Orkhis, is a former soldier who likes his football. Unlike some of her ex-boyfriends—mostly a pretentious lot of rich kids and nobles—you can have a proper chat over a beer with him. Even if he shows his American cards by calling football soccer.

The whole affair could be worse.

Still, I would rather be back on the base with my men than here dodging the floral arrangements and piles of fabric that seem to pop up everywhere.

Sitting at attention in my father's throne room, I wonder if I somehow got the time wrong for our meeting when my sister strolls in through the door.

"Father isn't coming," she says.

I stop myself just before rolling my eyes. Instead, I rise to my feet. "Then I think I will go find a way to be busy."

Following me out the door, Sarah stays close behind me. "Actually, here are a couple of things you could help me with."

I freeze and Sarah nearly rams into my back. I turn to steady her. It's then I get a good look at her. She seems shaky on her feet, her hand gripped in mine. If I am not mistaken, she is a little pale. Her dark brown eyes—the exact shade of my own—seem strained.

"Are you quite alright?"

She takes in a shallow breath through her nose and nods. "I am sure it is just my schedule getting the best of me. Father has been relentless. He is insisting I keep all of my regular engagements even though I am getting married the day after tomorrow."

That sounds like our father. He probably thinks it will make my sister look strong to our people. When we discovered she—and not her twin Henry—was heir to the throne a few months back, not everyone in Rhodon welcomed the change with open arms. While public opinion has softened somewhat thanks to the excitement of a royal wedding, our father will not stop until every person in our country accepts that Sarah will one day be queen.

Not for the first time, I am grateful my twin brother, Alex, and I were born a year after Sarah and Henry. There has never been any danger that the crown could land on my head.

I wrap an arm around Sarah's shoulder and squeeze her. She pats my hand and glances up at me.

"You can say no," she says. "But if you have any time, could you stop by the kitchen to make sure the cake baker is here and comfortable? She came from New York, and she's the one part of the wedding that Ryan and I were allowed to choose without . . ."

She trails off before saying it, but I know. The cake was the only part of the wedding our father gave up control on.

Sarah wobbles again, and I tighten my grip. "I can stop by the kitchen."

Her face lights up. I feel like a monster for hesitating to help for even a moment.

"You are the best brother ever." She leans up on her toes to kiss my cheek. "And if you ever tell Henry or James, I will say you are a liar."

Chuckling, I give her one more squeeze. "Are you sure you're okay?"

"Positive." She gives a weak smile. "But if I still feel poorly tomorrow, I will go to the doctor."

"Promise?"

"Promise."

She leaves me then for whatever our father has scheduled for her next. I briefly wonder what I would do in her shoes, but quickly dismiss the notion. For one, my feet are too big—and I have no interest in high heels—to ever fit in her literal shoes. As for the figurative? There is no point in considering what I would do if I were the future king.

I am not a superstitious person, but it seems like thinking about it just welcomes bad luck.

It takes me several minutes to make my way to the kitchen. With the sprawling palace my ancestors built, it can take half an hour to get from one end to the other. That is not the kind of home I would want for myself someday. If I ever move back to the city full-time, I would rather get my own place than set-up permanent residence here.

As I step into the kitchen, I nod at a footman leaving and take in the scene before me. About a dozen people in white chef's garb scramble about measuring cups of sugar and cracking open eggs. Though everyone is working at their own station, there is a rhythm to it all. And at the center of it is one woman.

She turns, and my breath catches. With thick, reddish-blonde hair piled into a bun on top of her head, skin the color of cream, and full lips painted red, she reminds me of a strawberry shortcake. My favorite dessert. Only, I bet she tastes better.

My gaze travels down her curves. Though it is hard to make out her form in the shapeless chef's wear, I can tell she has full hips and even fuller breasts. Both are the kind a man likes to hold onto as he buries himself inside of her.

My cock twitches at the thought.

If I had to guess, this would be the celebrity chef herself. For once I wish I watched reality TV so I could have seen the televised baking contest she won earlier this year.

I want to know everything about her. I need to know everything about her.

I take a step toward her just in time to watch as she catches her heel on the edge of the counter and flies forward.

TWO

NIKKI

I don't have time to scream as my feet fly up from under me. In a blur, my life flashes before my eyes. There's winning *Bake Your Sweets Off* earlier this year. Seeing my face on the cover of *People* magazine. Walking the red carpet at the Emmys. Pictures of my mother and dozens of her boyfriends I was supposed to call uncle.

They all rush through my head at lightning speed as I fall to my death.

I close my eyes, preparing for impact when two arms wrap around my back.

My eyes fly open again and stare into a pair of eyes the same color as the rich chocolate I used in the Buche de Noel that was my winning dish on *Bake Your Sweets Off*. They're set in a tan, concerned face covered in a light scattering of whiskers.

Either this man is a dark angel here to take me to some afterlife, or he is the most beautiful man I have ever come face to face with. I forget to breathe as my heart pounds in my chest.

"Are you okay?" my dark angel/savior asks.

Somehow, I bob my chin up and down as several more worried faces surround me. While I vaguely register them—and their cries for my safety—I am unable to tear my stare away from the man now holding me to his chiseled chest.

"Can you speak?" he asks.

I nod again, but also manage to let out a meek, "Yes."

His lips curve up one side, revealing the hint of a dimple. And as the blood rushes from my head to a certain part of my body, I am all too aware of how much I'd like to have my crew clear the room so I can give this man a proper thank you.

Which is so not what I should be doing here.

Shaking my head, I find my footing again. Feeling my cheeks flush dark red, I grab hold of the counter pretending to be interested in a crate of lemons.

"Thank you." I reach for a lemon in a poor attempt at normalcy. "I should have been paying more attention to where I was walking."

Just like I should be more careful of every step I take around this man who is practically oozing sexual pheromones. But like a moth drawn to a flame, I can't quite keep myself from casting him a sidelong glance.

He's resting a hip against the counter with an ease that tells me he's right at home here.

"Are you always in such a hurry?"

"Actually, yes." I grin then. "You don't win baking contests by going slow."

"But you also keep both feet on the ground."

"True." I sober quickly, realizing that with his smart suit and prim accent, this man is most likely a palace representative. Or, worse, a reporter sneaking into the palace for a fresh angle on his royal wedding story. "Is there something I can help you with? This is a closed kitchen."

His eyes crinkle around the edges, and I am once again struck with the urge to smile back or breathe into a bag. "I am here on behalf of the princess."

My stomach flutters. I'm not sure if it's the princess reference or his smoldering stare affecting the butterflies.

"Did the princess have any special requests?"

He shakes his head. "Just to make sure you have everything you need."

"Everything I need and more." I glance around the well-lit kitchen with every state-of-the-art appliance a baker could ask for—and more—at my disposal. "This is probably the best, most efficient kitchen I've worked in."

"Even better than your kitchen at home?"

"Oh, I don't own a bakery yet." Or even a kitchen at home. Or a home. "It has been such a whirlwind the past year, I've had pop-up bakeries around the U.S."

His dark eyebrows raise. "Do you like being away from home then?"

"I don't mind." There's no point telling him that I've never lived anywhere long enough to call it home. "It's good research to find the best place to eventually set up my shop."

He gives a short nod. His eyes narrow a second before his hand raises to my face. I jerk back instinctively and he pulls his hand back.

"You have a bit of frosting under your ear."

My hand flies up, and sure enough, I find a sticky dollop of sugar and butter.

My face flushes again. I hold up my finger. "Finding frosting in strange places. That's an occupational hazard for bakers."

"Sounds delicious." He takes my hand in his. The warmth from it radiates through me.

I wish I would have let him clear the frosting away with his own firm hands.

His gaze darkens as he brings my finger to his lips. He pulls my finger into his warm mouth. My whole body tingles as his tongue licks the frosting off.

Okay, I'd like to clear the room now. But that is dangerous thinking. Before I can recoil again, he drops my hand and grins.

"I was right," he says. "Delicious."

The flutters are back. "I'll have to save you a piece of cake later."

"You do that." He shoves his hands into his suit pockets. "Are you sure there isn't anything I can do to help you out?"

Asking him to fuck me until I can't stand probably doesn't fall under his job description. Even if it did, I can't lose track of why I'm here. To bake the best wedding cake any royal family has ever had and earn enough money to open my bakery.

"I'm good."

"I will see you around then." He winks. "Keep up the good work."

As soon as he is a few feet away, I can breathe again.

Lulu, one of my assistants, giggles as he leaves. "He's so charming. I think he's totally into you."

I shrug at that even as I bite back a grin. He really was charming. And he did seem to be flirting a little. Still, I can't get caught up in flirtations. I have a job to do. One that could set me up to finally have enough money to open my bakery without having to depend on loans.

"We need to make some more buttercream."

"But doesn't it seem like fate brought you and him here

together?" Lulu asks, still staring after him starry-eyed. "I mean, a man like that. In a royal palace. It's like a freaking fairytale."

"I don't believe in fairytales." And even though a handsome man just literally swept me off my feet, I'm not about to start. I hand her a whisk. "Now start stirring."

THREE

ALEX

I parry and thrust with a vigor and intensity that would make my childhood fencing instructor proud. I wish I was working up a sweat with a certain curvy baker, but trying to knock my brother on his ass is a decent enough substitute.

"Enough!" James cries out, tugging off his mask. His chest rising up and down. "Are you trying to kill me?"

"You would not be so out of breath if you spent a little more time in the gym instead of chasing women all over Oxford and London."

"And you wouldn't be so sexually frustrated if you spent a little more time using that other lance of yours on a fair maiden."

There is one woman I would not mind finding in my bed right now. But I can hardly admit that to my brother. For years, we have been trying to prove which one of us is right. I am not about to concede defeat now just because he is right on this front.

Instead, I cock my head to the side, my eyes narrow. "I suppose we have each found a way to sow our wild oats."

James grins. "My way is more fun."

I throw my mask at him. He narrowly dodges it, laughing in full force now. I am about to throw my lance at him too when the sound of heels clicking on the floor draws our attention to the door.

In walks the very woman who kept me up half of last night

"Oh." She glances between us. Confusion mars her otherwise perfect face. "I got turned around."

Interest crosses James's face, and I am once again struck with the urge to lance his face. "Where were you hoping to find yourself, gorgeous?"

I see red and take a step toward her, glaring at James. "Ms. Sommerset. What a pleasure to see you again. How about I help you?"

Correctly reading the situation, James steps back. While we may be embroiled in a lifelong competition to one-up each other, we have always respected one another's territory where women are concerned.

And though she may not realize it, Nikki Sommerset is mine. I very much intend to make her so before long.

Setting aside my lance, I offer her my arm. "I realized I did not properly introduce myself yesterday. I am Alex."

"Just Alex?" she arches an eyebrow.

"Just Alex."

"And what do you do here?"

I freeze mid-step. Is it possible she does not know who I am? Quickly recovering, I walk her back toward one of the main pathways in the palace.

"I am a captain in Rhodon's military."

"And they have you here working for the wedding?"

"Something like that." As far as my father is concerned, we are all of us always on duty. "Now about where you were going . . ."

She shakes her head. "I was trying to find my way back to the kitchen. The king asked me to bring samples of the cakes and desserts for tomorrow. I had a guy in a suit—a footman, I guess you'd call him—show me the way there, but I lost my guide."

"What did the king think of your samples?"

She lifts a shoulder. "I didn't even meet him."

That is not surprising. Though my father considers him a man of the people, he still manages to keep a distance between himself and them whenever possible.

Not wanting to let my father spoil this moment between Nikki and me—without even being here—I change the subject.

"What do you think of your time in Rhodon so far?"

"This palace is incredible." She grins at me, and it's like she's stroked my cock. "I've never been to a castle before."

I suppose it can be thrilling to someone who has not spent most of their life trying to get away from it. "How about the rest of the city?"

"Honestly, except for the trip from the airport, I haven't set foot outside of the grounds."

"That is a shame." And it is. Our ancient city is both vibrant and picturesque. Not to mention the mountains, beaches, and villages in our little island kingdom. It is unfortunate we are keeping Nikki so busy with the job that she has not had a moment to enjoy it.

Then I am struck with inspiration. "How long are you here?"

"I planned on sticking around a day or two after the wedding."

That is not much time, but I can make it enough. "I could show you around after the wedding."

She glances up at me, one of those red eyebrows arched. "Why would you do that?"

"It's the gentlemanly thing to do."

She rolls her eyes at that. "What's in it for you?"

I could tell her the pleasure of her company. But despite the ease in which we are speaking now, I get the feeling she might bolt if pressed too hard too fast.

"I hope you might do something for me in exchange." Before she can run, I cover her hand on my arm and tighten my hold. "Do you know, I am completely useless in the kitchen?"

"So are a lot of people."

"But a lot of people aren't in the presence of a world-famous baker." I squeeze her hand. "Perhaps you could give me a quick lesson."

Her mouth falls open as she gapes at me. Her full, red bottom lip practically begging me to bite it. "You want to learn how to bake?"

At this moment . . . "Certainly."

She chews on that very lip I imagined nibbling on myself, and my dick grows hard. What I would not give to have those same full lips wrapped around me. My dick twitches in response, and I push the thought out of my head. For now.

"I suppose I could give you a quick lesson after the rehearsal dinner tonight," she says.

The two of us would be alone in the kitchen after hours. "Sounds perfect."

I leave her at the door to the kitchen a few minutes later, my mood vastly improved. One baking lesson does not guarantee I will get Nikki into my bed. But contrary to my brother's earlier remarks, I can be very persuasive with women when I put my mind to it.

And I intend to put my full mind and body into getting more than a taste of this woman.

NIKKI

Alex dumps a cup of flour in a bowl, sending a mushroom cloud of dust into the air—and his face.

Biting back a grin, I cover his hand and show him how to pour the flour in without getting half of it all over his fancy clothes. Narrowing his eyes, and sticking his tongue out to the side, Alex tries it again and lands it perfectly.

"There you go!" I raise my hand and wait a few seconds for him to realize I'm offering him a high-five. "We'll make a baker out of you yet."

He obliges with a high five. He grabs my hand before it drops to my side and presses a kiss to it. "I have an excellent teacher."

My heart skips a beat, and I turn back to the ingredients, hoping to hide yet another telltale blush.

This evening has been surprisingly enjoyable. Though I nearly canceled the baking lesson with Alex at least a dozen times today, I'm glad I saw it through. With his jokes and easy manners, he's fun to be around.

Even if I want to drop my panties every time he's in the room.

After mixing the dry ingredients, we move on to the liquids. Alex combines them concentrating more than any other person I've ever seen.

I give the batter a quick stir and nod. "Perfect consistency."

He flashes a bright, proud smile, and my heart once again swells. Oh, he is bad news for me. I am not in a position to be losing my heart. Though, maybe what happens in Rhodon stays in Rhodon. A little vacation fling wouldn't be the worst thing in the world for me.

I shelve that idea for later as we fill the cupcake liners and put them in the oven.

"What now?" Alex asks.

"Now, we wait." We could make some frosting, but I have so much leftover from the wedding cake, it seems like a waste. Both in resources and in our time. "Tell me something about yourself."

He lifts a shoulder. "There's not much to say. I'm a helicopter pilot in the military. I'm here for the wedding."

It's a cagey answer for a man who spent the past half hour asking me about every moment of my life. He knows I went to four different high schools. That I spent one semester in college but dropped out to get a job to pay for it. That the job I took as an assistant to a pastry chef changed my life. How my life has been a whirlwind for the past year.

He knows everything except how much I'd like to let my guard down and have him kiss me until I can't think straight.

"Is it scary?" I ask, trying to come up with some sort of question to get him talking.

"Flying a helicopter or being a soldier?"

"Either. Both."

Sighing, he tugs off his apron, leaving him standing in a rolled-up white shirt and dress pants. He's never looked more delectable.

"I suppose it can be for some people."

"But not for you?"

He shakes his head. "I never feel more myself than when I'm doing something. The military gives me something to do."

"You're a regular man of action then, aren't you?"

His eyes flicker as he takes a step toward me. He places his hands on either side of my body, neatly trapping me against the counter. "You have no idea."

My breath catches a second before his lips capture mine in a searing kiss. My eyelids flutter shut as every part of me comes to life. I know I should put a stop to this before it gets out of hand. But while my head knows this, my hands reach up to his shirt and pull him closer.

Groaning, he nudges my lips open so his tongue can slide in. As it connects with mine, massaging it slowly, my body radiates with heat and need. That heat and need settle between my thighs.

That vacation fling sounds better and better.

He presses against me, his hard, thick cock rubs against my belly. My hand slides down to cup him. My fingers are just tracing his length when someone clears their throat, drawing me back to the moment.

Our mouths pull apart as we both look toward the source of interruption. It's the princess.

"Shit," I murmur, earning a grin from Alex.

Princess Sarah arches an eyebrow curiously. "I just came for a ginger ale."

She reaches into the refrigerator and pulls out a can. She starts back for the door but turns at the last minute. "Alex, if I had to say which one of my brothers I would find kissing the baker, you would've been my last guess."

Alex is her brother. She's a princess. The daughter of a king. That makes him . . .

My stomach drops. Slipping under his arm, I put as much distance between us as quickly as possible. Not only was I just caught making out on the job by my boss, which is so unprofessional. But it was with her brother. Who is a prince.

A mother-freaking prince. A prince sitting there smirking at me. The jerk. He must make it a habit of seducing the household staff.

The timer on the oven rings. I grab a potholder and pull the cupcakes out and set them on the counter harder than necessary.

"I should be going," I say.

His smirk turns into a frown. "You don't have to leave. My sister does not care. She's marrying her bodyguard for crying out loud."

So the whole family makes a practice of seducing the help. Sure, marriage is a little more serious than a fling. But I'm absolutely positive Prince Alex of Rhodon here is about as far away from dropping down to one knee and asking me to be his wife as I am to saying yes.

No way. Not happening. Not in this lifetime or the next.

"I have to get up early," I say as if that would've stopped me from having a fling with a hot soldier. But it will keep me from hopping into bed with a prince. "Baker's hours and all."

"I also get up early." He takes a step toward me, my heart pounding in my ears with every step closer he comes. "I'm a soldier."

"You're a prince."

"By birth. Not by choice."

I arch an eyebrow. "Do you get a say in the matter?"

He pauses mid-step a few feet away from me. His gaze darkens. "None of us chose to be born into nobility. We are all making the best of it that we can."

Which, I admit, is an interesting thing to say. Almost interesting enough to make me want to linger a little longer. Ask him a few more questions. But that curiosity will probably only end up with me lying flat on my back on the counter while a royal prince sows his wild oats.

That possibility—and the fact that I almost ended up in that very same position without knowing all the details—reignites my anger.

"As you know, I have to serve cake to a few thousand people tomorrow." I fold my arms over my chest. "I don't have time for your poor little royal boy sob stories."

His brows knit together. "Why are you angry?"

"I don't appreciate being lied to. If you don't have the decency to respect me enough with the truth, we're done here. Have a nice life."

With those parting words, I spin on my heel and stalk out the door. I pat myself on the back all the way to my rooms. Even as I do, my stomach flutters a little at the memory of his hands all over his body, his mouth on mine.

A handsome face and a smooth talker nearly turned me into putty. I would've given it all up—even put my job at risk —for a few steamy minutes. I am my mother's daughter.

FOUR

ALEX

As the music changes and the Rhodon Royal Choir's voices fill the cathedral, I rise to my feet.

James elbows me in the rib. "You might want to look a little like you want to be here, or the papers will have a hay day."

"Fuck the papers," I mutter under my breath, but I make more of a point to soften my expression.

Just because I am pissed off at the turn of events with Nikki, there is no reason for me to ruin my sister's wedding day. After everything she has been through this year, she deserves to be happy. Even if some of us are working on a serious case of blue balls.

My father and sister glide through the center of the church. With a bouquet clutched in her hands and a dress that probably weighs a hundred pounds, my sister stares forward. Though she decided not to wear a tiara today, with her chin raised and eyes resolute, she looks every inch a queen.

At the altar—where our Aunt Muriel, thank goodness, is not passed out—my sister's future husband gazes at her. His stare every bit as steady.

And when Sarah reaches Ryan's side, she takes his hands in hers. I can just see her mouth the words "I love you too."

I want that. Someone who both steadies me and lights a fire within my soul. Someone I can walk through life with knowing that everything will be okay because we are together.

And though she currently is not speaking to me—and may hate my guts—I think I have found that woman. I refuse to give her up without a fight.

NIKKI

I can't believe I didn't recognize a freaking prince when I saw one.

Luckily, with it being the wedding day, I have more than enough going on to spend too much time thinking much about Alex. Or where things could have gone if we hadn't been interrupted. And with it being his sister's wedding day, Alex has been too busy to go sniffing around the kitchen.

Thank goodness.

But even as I tell myself it's for the best, a small part of me can't help wishing I could go back to last night. Before I knew he was a prince. Back when he was a soldier, I was a baker, and the heat between us was off the charts.

Dressed in a simple black dress, I slip into the palace's ballroom to give the cake a final look before the princess and duke cut it. Glancing around, I feel like I'm being transported into a Disney movie. With flowers and candles everywhere, it is a real-life fairytale.

As if fairytales could ever be real life.

I know better.

I stay on the edge of the room making extra certain not to let my gaze slip to the head table, where I'm sure Alex is congratulating himself for being the first of his brothers to seduce the baker.

(I did a Google search on the family after our run-in and now know more about the royal family. I could pick any of them out of a line-up. I really should have done my homework sooner.)

I reach the cake and can't help smiling despite my foul mood. With layers stacked high and a waterfall of edible flowers cascading down the sides, this is a work of art.

"It's fit for a princess," a deep voice says behind me. Then Alex steps forward to stand at my side. "I've never seen a prettier cake."

I wait for the anger to come. Instead, warmth spreads through my belly. I sigh at myself and shake my head.

"We shouldn't be talking."

"Why not?"

"Because. I'm the help."

His expression grows dark. "You are an artist."

I try to ignore the way his words grab hold of my heart like a gentle caress. "You're a prince."

"I should have told you sooner." He runs a hand over his short, dark hair. "To be honest, it was refreshing having someone look at me like a person and not a title."

His words chisel away at my resolve to be mad at him. "I guess I can understand that."

"Forgive me?"

Sighing, I nod. Because who am I kidding? I'll never be

able to hold a grudge against this perfect specimen of a man. "I forgive you."

"Good." A smile breaks out across his face. He extends a hand. "Now, may I have this dance."

And just like that, the wall goes back up. "Are you crazy? You can't dance with me. You can call me an artist, but I'm still here as your family's employee."

His brows knit together, but after a moment he seems to come to a decision. Glancing over his shoulder, he takes my hand and leads me out the doors. Down the hallway, he stops suddenly and turns to me. He offers me his hand again.

"How about that dance?"

Try as I might, I just can't resist him. I lift my hand to his and rest my other hand on his shoulder. His arm goes around my waist, settling on the full curves of my hips. Another occupational hazard for a baker, I'm afraid. I always carry a few pounds around with me. A jolt of electricity zaps through me at his touch.

As a new song plays, muted only slightly by the doors, we move with the music. Alex leads with such authority and grace, it's no wonder he is both a soldier and a prince. They are so much a part of him in everything he does. Even dancing. I should have seen it sooner.

His head leans down until his lips are a breath away from my ear.

"I had a chance to try one of your pastries earlier today."

"Oh?" It's all I can manage to say with my heart thundering in my chest, my body tingling.

"It might be the sweetest thing I have ever tasted. Besides you. Nothing tastes as sweet as you."

He presses his lips just below my ear, like the flutter of a butterfly's wings. His mouth trails down my neck, and I melt.

Heaven help me, I can't fight him or this desire pulsing between us anymore.

"Let me have you." His low whisper rumbles in my belly, stoking the hot coals already burning in there. "Have me."

I nod, unable to form the words even as my lips find his.

This time, our kiss is like an explosion. My hands slide up and around his neck. His hand moves down to cup my ass, pulling me to him again. My body melts against him. He's rock hard, his need for me every bit as strong as mine.

He presses my back against the wall, and his other hand roves up my thigh leaving goosebumps in its wake. His thumb slides under the satin of my panties and finds me. I am already wet for him. I instinctively move against him, sighing.

Alex pulls back suddenly. My eyes fly open as I slide down his body.

"Not here," he says. "Fuck, I'd love nothing more than to take you here. But I want to be the only one he sees you come."

Taking my hand again, Alex strides down the hall with me racing to keep up with him. After a few turns around corners I'll never remember, he opens another door and pulls me inside. He slams the door shut and pushes me against it. His hands mold over my curves, and I hold on tight to him as he kisses me again.

I can't wait any longer. I tear my mouth away from him

"I need you inside of me. Now."

My hands move down, reaching for the button of his pants. I pull out his hard length, massaging him with my hand as he groans.

"Wait," he says. "I need a condom."

"I'm on the pill. And I'm clean and good to go."

He nods. "Same here."

With one swift yank, he tears the crotch of my panties and lifts me as he slams into me.

I cry out as my body stretches to accommodate his size. "Oh, God."

"You feel so good." His breath tickles my neck as his cheek presses against mine.

Then he moves, pumping in and out, faster and faster. His hands and fingers gliding over me, building the pleasure inside of me.

Just as I am not sure I can take it anymore, that pleasure explodes inside of me. Alex pushes in once more, shouting my name as his cum shoots inside of me.

My breath is short and labored as my heart slows. Cradling me in his arms, making me feel cared for and protected for the first time in my life, Alex kisses my hair.

"Stay with me?"

I nod, because really, where else can I go when my body is already crying out for him again?

FIVE

ALEX

I wake to an empty bed the next morning. Even after spending several hours lingering over each other's bodies, it seems Nikki is forever a baker who wakes with the sun. Growing up, I was always the earliest riser of my family. That habit suits me well in the military. It seems I have competition.

Stretching, I grin at that thought and slide out of the bed. I pull on a fresh pair of briefs and dig out some clothes. Now that the wedding is over, and the social obligations are done, I tug on a pair of jeans and a button-up shirt—just to appease my father in case I run into him today.

There is only one person I want to run into—and around with—today. I have a pretty good idea where she is right now.

Nikki and her crew have nearly finished cleaning the kitchen when I arrive. I stand at the doorway, unnoticed, watching the way she moves about. In total command of the room and everyone in it, she is somehow everywhere at once.

Helping to wash the last of the dishes, freezing the top layer of the wedding cake, showing an assistant the best way to arrange a plate of pastries. She does it all so effortlessly, yet methodically.

It reminds me of the way she was in bed last night.

The memory of those hands on me—of her taste—makes me hard.

Almost as if she senses me and my thoughts, Nikki's gaze meets mine. Her cheeks flush an appealing shade of pink.

"Hey, everyone," she calls out, bringing the room to a standstill. "You can take a fifteen-minute break."

I arch my eyebrow.

"Make that twenty minutes."

I smirk, and her cheeks darken even more. "Let's just call it a solid thirty."

If anyone wonders why they're being given a break when they're so close to finishing, they don't say it. They're all either too polite or too well trained, to question their boss.

Once we're alone, I stride toward her, where she's still gripping a dish towel between her hands.

"Good morning," I say, placing my hands on either side of her on the counter.

She swallows. "Good morning."

"I missed you when I woke up."

"I had work to do."

"So I see."

"It still needs finishing."

"It can wait until I've kissed you good morning."

She drops the towel and pulls me toward her as my hands grab hold of her hips. Our mouths collide, and then our tongues as our hands rove over each other's bodies.

My mouth moves to her neck, sucking and nibbling as my fingers move to unbutton her white chef's coat. My lips follow where my fingers have been. Stroking, urging, teasing. When I've reached the last button, I push the coat off of her shoulders and reach for the back of her bra. Once her large, full breasts are freed, my mouth covers one of her nipples.

She gasps out, her hands gripping my neck. Urging me on. My fingers slip to the button of her jeans, pushing them to the floor along with her panties.

I continue to suckle on her as I reach for the back of her thighs, lifting her so her bare ass sits on the counter.

"This is hardly sanitary," she murmurs.

I pull back a fraction. "Clearly, I am not doing my job properly if you can think about kitchen sanitation."

I give her nipple a flick and she cries out in pleasure as I drop to my knees, pulling her toward me. My thumbs part her fold, and I bring her pussy to my mouth. Her breathing quickens, and my fingers dig into her smooth hips as my lips and tongue suck on the very sweetness of her core. Her hand flies out to grip the counter, knocking a bowl to the ground.

I spare a glance at the bowl and smirk. Perfect. Reaching over, I swipe a dollop of frosting on my finger and trail it up the inside of her thigh to her clit. She wriggles at the stickiness.

"Hold still, baby." My tongue and my follow the path painfully slow, lapping up the vanilla frosting and Nikki. Two of my favorite flavors. Every inch I move, the more frantic she becomes. The harder my cock gets.

I can never get enough of her.

I'll never have enough of her.

She has wedged herself permanently into my heart and soul.

"Alex!" she calls out as her thighs press against my face and she tumbles over the edge into sweet ecstasy.

She falls back against the island, her breasts rising up and down with her breath. I rise to my feet, my hands sliding up her hips. Tugging my T-shirt over my head, I unbutton my jeans and pull my cock out. She eyes me hungrily as I pump myself once and line up at her entrance.

Pushing up to her elbows, she licks her lips as I thrust into her.

She calls my name once more, and then I lose all sense of everything but the way she feels as I become one with her. And as I lead us both to completion, my heart pounds in my chest for her. Only for her.

SIX

NIKKI

Alex was right. We needed the full thirty minutes.

After he made me come three times, we barely had time to re-dress and clean-up the bowl of buttercream I accidentally sent flying in a fit of passion.

Once the crew and I have the kitchen back in pristine condition, I eye the room with some remorse. In the past year, I've worked in some of the best restaurants in the United States and Europe. None of them hold a candle to the palace. And even though I'll finally have enough to set up my shop once this check clears, I wonder if it will live up to this.

I wonder if anything can after the way Alex and I just christened this place.

Taking my hand, Alex leads me to a waiting motorcycle. Handing me a helmet, he straddles it. "Hop on."

My belly flutters as I follow his orders. Wrapping my arms around his waist, I hold on as the bike comes to life and we take off through the streets of Rhodon. We drive around for some time, historical buildings flying by along with the modern odds and ends that make a city exciting. Restaurants. Galleries. Bakeries.

As we travel the streets, my heart soars taking in every sight, sound, and scent I can.

We come rounding back through the town center and Alex brings his motorcycle to a stop. Throwing down the kickstand, he climbs off and offers me his hand. I grin at him like a fool as he helps me off. Leaving our helmets on the motorcycle, he holds my hand and walks with me to an empty storefront.

"What do you think?" he asks.

Looking it over, I can see that while the building itself is probably hundreds of years old, someone has recently done major renovations. With the large windows papered over, I can imagine just how much natural light must come in through them. The cobblestone road around it and the unobstructed view of the castle make it perfectly charming.

"It's great. What's it going to be?"

His eyes brighten. "I want to buy it for you."

I shake my head. "Wait, what?"

"This store. I want to buy it for you, so you can start your bakery."

My heart jolts. "So I can start my bakery. In Rhodon."

He nods. He holds both of my hands up to his lips and kisses them.

"You will be a hit. I know it." His face shines with excitement. "We can get an apartment—or maybe a townhouse nearby—so you can get to work early every morning. I will find work of my own here. I have served my king and country long enough."

He continues, telling me all about the places we can go together. With every word, the panic inside of me grows.

Memories of my childhood. Of moving for men. Of broken hearts. Of starting over. It all swirls around with the panic, becoming bigger and bigger until it bursts.

"I can't move here."

His face falls. "Okay. You want a bakery in the states. We can make that work. I am not the heir, after all. I can live wherever I want."

I shake my head, pulling my hands away from his.

"I can't be with you. Not here. Not anywhere."

His jaw tightens. "May I ask why not?"

I shake my head, which is still spinning from everything he's said.

"This has been fun, but I have to go." And before he can say anything that changes my mind, I run down an alley. I keep running until I'm out of breath. Then, and only then, do I get control of my fears. And as I do, the tears fall down my cheeks.

SEVEN

ALEX

I am at least three or four fingers into a bottle of some of our father's finest Scotch when James finds me brooding in an empty dayroom.

"Whoa," he says. "Who died?"

Just my hopes and dreams for the future. "I'm not in the mood."

"So I see." James drops into the seat next to me. He places a hand on my shoulder. "I'll repeat the question. Who died?"

Not wanting to answer, I shrug his hand away. "I'm heading out tomorrow."

"Is this about the baker?"

"How do you know about Nikki?"

"Anyone with eyes can see the way you've been hanging around her the past few days." He smirks. "And those of us with good eyes noticed the two of you leave the wedding reception last night without coming back."

"It was just a bit of fun."

Wasn't that what Nikki said? That we were just having fun, but she couldn't be with me.

"Doesn't look like you're having much fun now."

"Go to hell."

James chuckles at that and reaches for the bottle. He sniffs, grimaces, and then pours himself a small snifter of it. He tosses back a swig and fills the glass again.

I glare at him. "What are you doing?"

"Getting on your level so we can talk about this."

"You don't have to get on my level," I grumble. But I hold out my glass and wait for him to give me a refill. We sit in silence, nursing our drinks, for a few more minutes.

Eventually, I sigh. There's no point in avoiding the conversation. He will just stay until I tell him.

Filling him in on the details, I leave out some of the parts that happened behind closed doors. But as my twin, there is no one in the world I trust more with knowing everything else. He listens in silence until I reach the end.

"I fell in love with her. I asked her to stay here with me."

"As in you would be staying here, too?" After I nod, he releases a low whistle. "Giving up your military career for a woman. I never thought I would live to see the day."

She's worth it. At least I thought so.

"Love gives you crazy ideas. Makes you do stupid things."

"You can say that again." James takes another drink then sets his glass down. "Do you think love might be making her do stupid things too?"

"How do you figure?"

"Like maybe falling for a prince in a couple of days is scary for her." He shrugs. "A lot of women are fine spending a night or two with a prince, but settling down with one is not for the faint of heart."

Anger rises fast and hot inside of me. "Are you saying

she's one of those women looking for a quick fumble with a prince?"

"Not in the least. But this life is still a lot to take on." He lifts a shoulder. "Maybe you should find her. Ask her what's going on. And really listen."

Everything he says makes sense. "I could do that."

Her plane isn't scheduled to leave for a couple more days, which gives me time.

"If you love her as much as you say, you owe it to yourself and her." James pats me on the back. "But wait till you sober up. Right now you smell like a cheap—"

"It's an expensive bottle."

James wrinkles his nose. "You still smell like shit."

NIKKI

When the crowned princess of Rhodon invites me for a meeting a few hours after I left Alex, I know it can't be good.

It's my own damn fault for crossing the professional line and getting excessively personal with my client's brother. Who, as if I need reminding, is a prince. A prince I rejected without giving a reason.

I'll be lucky if I get out of this country without a bounty on my head.

After waiting in the pale blue sitting room for what feels like forever, the door swings open. A footman steps inside followed immediately by the princess. She slides into the seat next to mine and meets my gaze.

Okay. I can't take it anymore.

"I'm sorry. I didn't mean to break your brother's heart." I hold up my hand to keep her from speaking, which is probably breaking some sort of royal protocol. But at this point, who cares? I've broken all kinds of rules—both royal and my own—since getting here. "In my defense, if you knew what my childhood was like, you would understand why I had to end it."

Sarah's brows remain frozen in their upright and lock position. "Your childhood?"

Sighing, I ball my hands into fists on my knee. "My dad left when I was a baby. After that, my mom was always convinced her real Prince Charming was just around the corner."

She fed me so many lies and stories pulled straight from storybooks. "Every time she met a man who she thought was 'the one,' we'd move in with him. I'd get pulled into another school. Sometimes another town. Within a year, they'd call it quits. We'd be out on our own, and she'd be brokenhearted."

"That must have been difficult." Princess Sarah gives me a tight-lipped grin. "That would put a lot of people off love."

"Like you wouldn't believe." Now that the floodgates are open—and she seems so sympathetic—I can't seem to stop. "By the time I was four or five, I knew how to make dinner. Nothing much, but at least enough to keep us fed. When my mother should've been nursing my scraped elbows and knees, I was getting her up off the floor every time a man broke her heart."

I shake my head. "I never felt like I belonged anywhere or to anyone. Not until I found baking."

A single tear slips down my cheek. I wipe it away furiously. I'm not a crier. I won't do it again today. "I promised myself that if I ever had the means to set up a bakery, I would do it. On my own. And I would never, ever, under any circumstances let myself think there are such things as happily ever afters where men are concerned."

I let out a shaky breath. "I know you're a princess and all, but I don't believe in fairy tales."

Princess Sarah lets out a little laugh. "You know, I didn't believe in fairy tales either. Not until I met Ryan. Loving him, having him love me, changed that. It makes me stronger."

Panic slices through me. "But aren't you afraid it could all go away?"

"If I was it wouldn't matter." She lifts a shoulder. "I don't know your mother or what you've been through. But when you find love—real love—you have to get past the fear of it going away. Otherwise, you miss out on something magical."

What she's saying makes sense. I can see that rationally. But erasing a lifetime of watching my mother's heartache isn't easy to do.

"I care about your brother. Deeply." I shake my head. "I don't know how it happened. And so fast. I'm usually so smart about men."

"You can be smart and in love." The princess reaches out and covers my hand. "For what it's worth, I love all of my brothers dearly. They are some of my best friends. I do not know how I could have gotten through this life without them."

My gaze lifts to hers. She gives my hand a gentle squeeze. "But while I know I can count on and depend upon all of my brothers, there is no one I would trust more than Alex."

"Because he's a soldier?"

"He is a great soldier. But he is a better man. The kind who will not let you down."

I choke on a sob. "Are you saying I should give a relationship with him a chance? Is that why you brought me here?"

"Honestly? I wanted to thank you for giving me the most beautiful wedding cake. And I was hoping you would sign this for me." She opens her purse and pulls out a copy of my season of *Bake Your Sweets Off*. "But if you're asking my opinion, I think you need to get your heart and head together and listen to what both have to say."

And as my cheeks flush red, the crowned princess of Rhodon throws her arms around me and pulls me into a hug. "On a personal note, I have always wanted a sister. Now more than ever."

EIGHT

ALEX

My feet hit the pavement as I think about what Alex has said. When Nikki pushed me away—ran away—it was not anger or disgust in her tone. It was fear. I was just too busy feeling sorry for myself to see that.

Once it is a reasonable hour, I will find her—wherever she is—and ask her what is going on and listen. If it turns out she is afraid of a life tied to a royal, I will help her see that she does not have to be afraid of a future with me. And, I will leave the royal family if I must. All that matters is her.

Surprisingly better at holding my liquor than James, I'm up the next morning with the sun and out the door for a run. I've never been one to sit and wait, and the run will give me time to burn

I am also apparently a glutton for pain. Because when I reach the corner that leads me to where Nikki left me yesterday or another route, I head toward the bakery. As I do,

I notice someone seated on a bench outside of it. As I draw closer, my breath catches as my pace slows to walk.

I would recognize that person anywhere. Because she is the person who has stolen my heart. And it is hers to keep no matter what.

Catching sight of me for herself, Nikki stands. In her hands, she holds a small box.

"I was hoping I'd find you here." She swallows hard. "Your sister told me you run this way when you're in town."

So she's been talking to my sister, has she? We will come back to that later.

"You are up early."

"Baker's hours. I brought pastries." She sets the box back on the bench and faces. "I'm sorry I ran away without talking to you yesterday. Not only did I probably twist my ankle, but I didn't give you a reason."

I nod. "I'll listen."

"Someday I'll tell you the full story. But right now, all that matters is I was scared. So I ran."

"I get the fear." I move toward her and grip onto her shoulders, pleased when she leans toward me instead of away. "I know this life isn't for everyone. I know I'm a lot to take on."

She frowns at that. "I'm not afraid of you or your life. I'm afraid of what will happen to me if I forget about my own."

I shake my head. "I never want you to think your life and dreams are any less important than mine or anyone else's."

"I see that now." She hesitates a moment then lifts her hand to my cheek. "I . . . didn't have a very good example of love growing up. I'm not sure I'll be any good at it. But if you're willing to show me the way, I'm a quick learner."

My heart swells in my chest. "I love you, Nikki Somerset."

"And I love you." She gives a shaky laugh. "I've never said that to anyone before. I love you."

"Then I'm all the more honored."

I wrap my arms around her waist and bring her lips to mine. It is our first lesson in love already. Every disagreement can be solved with a conversation and a kiss. And while we both have a lot to learn and navigate in the years ahead, I am willing and able to give it my all.

We both are worth that kind of love.

EPILOGUE

NIKKI

four months later

Alex carries in the newspaper on a silver tray with two glasses of orange juice, coffee service for two, and a pile of toast for us to share. Even after more than four months of living at the palace, I'm not sure I'll ever get used to having someone deliver my breakfast in bed.

As I steal an appreciative look at Alex's bare, muscular chest with just a hint of hair trailing under his boxer briefs, I'm also not sure I'll ever get used to the fact that I'm in love with an honest to God prince. More—he's crazy in love with me too. Sometimes that love still scares me, but it also makes me stronger and better. Just like Sarah said it would.

Catching my stare, Alex smirks.

"Like what you see?"

"Always."

Setting my cup of juice on my nightstand, he presses his lips to my temple before sliding back into bed next to me. He fills the cups with coffee adding two sugars and a splash of cream to my cup—just the way I like it. The way he treats me, I'd feel like a princess even if we weren't living in a palace for the moment.

I'm taking my first sip when he slides the paper to me.

I arch an eyebrow. "What's this?"

"You might want to flip to the front page of the lifestyle section."

My heart skips a beat. "You mean . . ."

Not waiting for me to recover from the shock, Alex slides out the section in question and holds it open. There, in full cover on the front page, above the fold, is my face. I'm doing the stupid pose all bakers seem to do when they're photographed in their kitchens—arms folded with a hip leaning against a prep station, organized chaos behind me.

"You look gorgeous."

I dismiss Alex's compliment and reach for the paper with shaking hands. In addition to my portrait, there are a handful of others showing the front of my new bakery, which officially opens tomorrow. As a favor to the crowned princess, I agreed to give Rhodon's biggest newspaper an early preview to drum up good press for the family.

Now, here it is—in black and white and, well, color. My first bakery's first review. And even though the headline sounds positive—"Celebrity Baker's New Place is All Sweet" —I can't quite bring myself to read the rest.

I shove the paper at Alex. "You read it. Summarize it for me. Please."

Shaking his head at me, but sparing me a playful wink, Alex does just that. I feel like the ocean is roaring in my ears, but I pick up a few phrases.

"Somerset's confections are divine—even without a royal connection . . ."

". . . a must-stop for every Rhodonian with a sweet tooth . . ."

". . . no doubt, Somerset Bakery will be a staple for years to come."

Setting down the paper, Alex grips my chin and raises it.

"I'm so proud of you, babe." He presses a quick kiss to my lips. "I never had a doubt."

No, he didn't. Even after I insisted on securing my own financing for the bakery space he showed me, Alex never pouted. Instead, he threw himself into being my biggest cheerleader and supporter while I set up the shop. While there were a few hiccups along the way—a busted sewer pipe and some shoddy construction from a previous tenant—it really came together.

And with the love of my life there with me every step of the way, I feel like I've been living a dream.

I raise my left hand to cup his cheek, my new engagement ring sparkling in the morning light. "I couldn't have done it without you."

"You will never be without me again." He turns his face to kiss my palm. Then he takes my hand in both of his, smiling down at the ring he put on my hand just two days ago. "Now that we are officially engaged, we should look at getting our own place."

He grins, but a dark shadow falls over his eyes.

I know he's worried about James. His brother has been in the United States the past week for an economic forum, filling in for their sister who didn't want to travel overseas at this point in her pregnancy. But no one has heard from him in more than twenty-four hours. Alex has tried to wave it off, saying his twin is probably on a bender, but he can't fool me.

I squeeze Alex's hand. "I'm sure we'll hear from him soon."

"I'm sure." Then his grin brightens. "Let's not worry about that right now. I think we have some celebrating to do."

As his hand slides up my thigh and under the silk of my nightgown, I am all agreement. I have finally found my place in this world. And thanks to my prince, I'm living a freaking fairytale. Happily ever after and all.

JAMES

RIDICULOUSLY ROYAL #3

ONE

JAMES

The phone buzzes on my nightstand. Before I even open my eyes, I can tell today is going to royally suck.

For one, my mouth feels like it has a wool sock shoved inside of it. And, the last time my head hurt this badly, my rowing team at Oxford had just won the Royal Cup. We had all gone on a two-day bender. By the time we finally crashed, we all swore we would never get that pissed again.

It would seem I broke that promise last night.

On top of that, I am rock hard. The last time I was this hard without relief, I . . . . Come to think of it, I cannot remember a time my cock was this hard. With or without a beautiful woman's help. And there is never a shortage of beautiful women when you are the King of Rhodon's youngest son.

A body stirs in the bed next to me, and a grin spreads across my lips. Perhaps today will not be as bad as predicted.

I just need to pop some Tylenol, chug a bottle of water, and I'll be ready to work out one of my situations.

My eyes squint against the light. As my vision clears, my smile grows brighter.

Jackpot. The woman lying next to me is stunning. With long, blonde hair that falls in waves over her shoulders, her skin is like strawberries and cream. Long eyelashes fan over high cheekbones.

With her wearing only a lacy bra and panty set, I have a full view of her curvy body. Full hips, fuller tits, and an ass I would like to examine more closely. My fingers long to begin their full study of her body, but first things first. I should find out how she likes her eggs prepared.

Pity I don't remember much beyond meeting her last night.

The phone rings again. Groaning, I flip over to reach for it and frown.

"What the . . . ?"

There's a thin gold band on my left hand. It was not there last night. Come to think of it . . . I sit up to take a better look at my surroundings. This is not my hotel room in New York City. Where I am supposed to be attending a world economic forum on the king's behalf.

Then I catch a glimpse of the Las Vegas strip outside the window.

"Bloody hell." My father is going to have my neck when he finds out I am in Las Vegas. With a gold ring on my left hand. A gorgeous stranger in my bed. And a hangover the size of the royal family's treasury.

Forget having my neck. My father will have my head—and my dick. And, to make matters worse, my wife is an American. He still has not gotten over the fact that two of his children have already settled down with Americans. The news that I—his favorite—have done just that, will give him a heart attack.

And the last thing my sister—the future queen, who is currently in the hospital with severe morning sickness—needs is a premature coronation.

I can practically see the headlines now.

The Royal Screw-Up Strikes Again

I swear loudly before I can stop myself. The woman next to me jerks awake. Her eyes fly open. She blinks furiously as she pushes herself upright.

Then she comes face to face with me. Now the hazy memories become a bit more clear. I met her at a bar after the forum. She was wearing a smart blazer and had her hair tucked into a tidy bun. After that, it gets blurry again. I want to say her name is Melissa . . . No, Alyssa.

"Morning," I say dryly. "Fancy a cup of tea."

She covers her mouth, barely masking a scream.

"What . . . where . . . who . . ." She shakes her head. "What's going on?"

I spot the gold band on her own left hand and sigh. "It would appear, my dear, that we are husband and wife."

Her emerald green eyes widen as I hold my hand next to hers.

She gasps and clutches her head in her hands. "Oh, I thought it was a dream."

"So, you remember?"

"Vaguely." She shakes her head and winces. Apparently, I am not the only one with a headache. "How did we get here?"

"That sounds like a conversation for breakfast." I reach for my phone, which is ringing once more. "If you'll excuse me, I need to take this."

For some reason, my *wife's* sincere shock comforts me.

Unless she is the world's greatest actress, I at least do not have to worry she is a fortune hunter looking to bag a prince.

Closing the door to the bedroom behind me and stepping into a living room area, I take the call from my oldest brother Henry.

"Do you have any idea what time it is here?" I ask, noting that it is just after five local time.

"Do you have any idea where you are?" Henry asks. "You ditched your security detail and never made it to your room last night."

"I needed a break from the meetings," I lie. "You know how dry they can be."

I hear Henry's heavy sigh through the speaker. "Who is the girl?"

"What makes you think a woman is involved?"

"You have been out of communication for the better part of a day. Of course, a woman is involved."

I cannot fault his logic. Particularly since it is spot on. And, to be honest, I am not sure I can fix this on my own.

"Look, I screwed up. But I am going to fix it." I take a deep breath. "Could you possibly run interference?"

He sighs again. "How much time do you need?"

"A day." I hope that is enough to get an annulment. It seems that if you can get married in minutes in Vegas, you should be able to get un-married quickly too.

"I will do my best. But you owe me." More than Henry will ever know I hope. "I hope she was worth it."

I wish I could remember if she was.

TWO

ALYSSA

Almost the second the bedroom door closes behind James, I release the breath I was holding. There's nothing like a jolt of fear to wake you up from a booze-infused sleep. Here's hoping the adrenaline will last long enough to ride out the worst of the hangover.

What the heck happened last night?

One minute, I was sidling up to Prince James of Rhodon at a bar hoping to overhear some juicy gossip that I could text back to my editor. The next, he was offering to buy me a shot.

Me. A lowly research assistant at a trashy gossip magazine.

And so, even though I was on the clock, I said sure.

From there, things escalated quickly. Snapshots of several more rounds of shots and a bottle or two of champagne come to mind. Then I vaguely remember pulling up my magazine's travel app and booking us tickets on the next plane to Vegas. I remember getting on the plane and then nothing. Just waking up this morning with a freaking wedding ring on my finger and the need to puke or pee really badly.

I sure picked a hell of a time to get blackout drunk for the first time.

If any of the reporters I grew up idolizing could see me now, they'd revoke my journalism license on the spot and tell me to find a new job. Which would really suck, because I still have a mountain of student loan debt to pay off just for earning that degree. And if my parents back in Nebraska knew what I was up to, they'd have our whole church praying for me around the clock.

I'm way out of my element. I see that now. It's my first real in-the-field assignment. And based on the number of text messages and missed calls from Ned, my boss, it's probably my last.

Sneaking into the bathroom with my phone, I empty my bladder and double-check to make sure the door is locked.

Taking in a few deep breaths, I brace myself for the worst and return Ned's latest call. He answers on the first ring.

"The next words out of your mouth better be 'I'm with the prince right now' or your ass is fired."

"I'm with the prince right now." Oh, God. I can't believe those words just came out of my mouth.

There's a moment of silence while Ned probably picks his jaw up off the floor. "You're kidding, right?"

"Not even a little."

At least if I get fired for this, I'll have the most insane story to tell for the rest of my life.

"So that's why you booked a plane to Las Vegas late last night? To travel with the prince's entourage."

Apparently.

"The prince said he was going. He asked if I wanted to come along. There wasn't time to ask, so I booked a flight."

There's a fifty percent chance that the story is true.

"Good thinking. That kind of hustle is exactly what will get you ahead at our publication. Especially if you come up with an exclusive angle."

"Oh, my angle is about as exclusive as it gets."

Especially if it turns out I am in fact married to the prince. I don't actually have any recollection of walking down the aisle or exchanging vows. For all I know, the prince and I are kleptomaniacs who stole his and her wedding bands from an unsuspecting couple.

"Can you give me another day to follow up on this?" I ask.

"Sure thing. Just answer your phone next time. And Alyssa?"

"Yes, sir?"

"Keep this up and you'll have your own beat in no time."

Ned hangs up before I can respond. Planting my hands on the counter, I take another couple of breaths as I stare at my reflection in the mirror.

This is easily the most irresponsible thing I've ever done. Times a hundred.

I briefly think of Mr. Darcy, my tuxedo cat, who is probably waiting for me at home. Fortunately, thanks to the crazy hours I often keep, I invested in an automatic feeder, water fountain, and self-cleaning litter box a few months ago. While he might be angry when I get home, at least he'll be fed and clean.

On the other side of the door, I hear shuffling. My hubby must be done with his own phone call. I could always just stay in here until he leaves. Then I can slip out never to see him again. Until he inevitably decides to marry one of the models or actresses he's frequently pictured with, and he needs to track down his accidental wife.

Or I could be a grown-up and face the consequences of too much tequila and bubbly.

Pulling on a robe, I brace myself and open the door.

The prince has pulled on his pants and has his white shirt on, but unbuttoned. I try not to stare at his rock hard abs or the tiny trail of hair that disappears under his waistband.

He glances up. "It is Alyssa, right?"

I nod. "James?"

"You've got it." He grins. "We probably have a lot to discuss, but could we do it over breakfast? I would kill for a plate of hash browns."

"Sure."

I reach for my own pants and shirts keeping watch of him out of the corner of my eye. He's acting so ordinary. You'd think a prince who just found himself married to a reporter would be a little more upset.

Unless . . . is it possible he doesn't remember who I am? If that's the case, I could really maybe get out of this whole situation relatively unscathed.

THREE

JAMES

I almost groan with pleasure as I take my first bite of hash browns drowned in sausage gravy. My father might think Americans are less civilized, but they know how to do breakfast right.

My twin's girlfriend introduced me to the haystack a few months ago. I will never be able to see another potato without wishing it was shredded, fried, and drowned in gravy, eggs, and meat. I feel a twinge of guilt in my gut at the thought of James. I have at least a dozen unanswered calls and texts from him on my phone. But as he, like Sarah, is actually living in the palace right now, I cannot risk having my father intercept my messages.

I will just have to trust Henry to call off the dogs and make sure everyone believes that I am alive.

"So, Alyssa," I say after taking a few bites. "You're from New York?"

Her fork freezes an inch from her mouth. "Do you really want to do the whole first date talk?"

"It seems appropriate since we're most likely married."

"Oh, we're married." She sets her fork down and reaches for her phone. She punches in a few buttons and hands it to me. "See that charge? It's for a twenty-four-hour wedding chapel."

I wince. "I suppose it is all the more reason to get to know each other."

Her jaw drops. "You don't really want to stay married, do you?"

"No, I think not. But we can still be friends."

Now she laughs. "Friends. I don't know where you live, and you don't know what I do for a living."

"Touché." Relief washes through me. She really does not know who I am. "Okay. I propose a truce. You do not ask me about my real life, and I repay the favor."

"That seems fair." If I am not mistaken, she looks equally relieved. "Okay, it's a deal."

"Deal." I start to take another bite but pause. "I should probably apologize for getting us into this mess."

She starts. "Why? I don't remember anyone holding a gun to my head and forcing me on an airplane."

"So you do remember last night?"

She shrugs. "Bits and pieces."

"Same." And for the first time, we share a grin. "Do you know how we got here?"

"I am pretty sure I put it on my company credit card."

"And the wedding?"

"That one is on my personal card."

"I will reimburse you for both. I have the resources," I finish lamely.

We fall silent a moment, then Alyssa pulls out her phone.

"I did some research. From what I can tell, as long as neither of us objects, we can sign the paperwork later today and have everything go through within twenty-four to seventy-two hours."

I have to admit, I'm impressed. When did she have time to do all this research? I barely had my wits about me to get dressed and order a car. "You are a regular detective."

She flinches at my words. Have I hit upon a nerve? I shrug off the thought, because hopefully in twenty-four to forty-eight hours, this will all be behind us.

Oddly enough, that thought gives me a twinge of disappointment. There can be no future for us. But if circumstances were different, I would want to get to know this gorgeous, unpretentious woman tucking into a plate of waffles across from me.

I am momentarily distracted by the whipped cream on her lips. I would like to taste it—both the lips and the cream. Which is not the thought a man should be having toward the woman he accidentally married.

Unfortunately, my dick has never particularly listened to my brain.

Alyssa catches my grin. "What?"

I shake my head. "It's nice to eat with someone who shares my affinity for breakfast foods."

"Let me guess, you usually share your breakfast with women who order cups of hot water with a side of lemon on the side."

She has a sarcastic streak to her. I like that.

"But I never married any of them."

She just shakes her head at that. No, out of all the beautiful women who have been on my arm, none of them ever tempted me to drop to one knee and propose. Yet something about the woman across from me prompted me to do just that.

She is beautiful and funny. But there must be more. I wonder if I will have the opportunity to find that out while we do damage control.

ALYSSA

James asks the Taxi driver to drop us off a block away from the wedding chapel. I'm not surprised. While he hasn't been recognized—yet—I imagine he wants to avoid as much of a trail of witnesses as possible.

Besides, after gorging myself on a waffle, hash browns, and eggs, I could use the exercise, such that it is.

When we set foot inside the chapel. With pink walls, an over-the-top chandelier, and the gaudiest fountain I've ever seen, the place screams of vintage Vegas. And tackiness.

Before I can stop it, a giggle bubbles out of me. James turns toward me confusion plainly written on his face. I cover my mouth with my hand to keep another laugh from coming out.

I snort instead.

James gives a short laugh of his own. "What's so funny?"

"It's just this place," I say in a whisper, in case the owner is lurking nearby. "I can't believe *this* was my wedding venue."

"Not what you dreamed about when you were a little girl, hmm?"

"I wasn't one of those girls who had my whole wedding planned out." Though, I did flip through the occasional bridal magazine when my best friend in college got engaged. "I just always figured when the time came, I would get married somewhere less . . ."

"Pink?"

I snort again, and cover my mouth with both hands, eyes wide in horror.

Chuckling at me, James takes me by the elbow and guides me toward the counter. The man seated behind it brightens.

"You came back!" He steps around the counter to take both of our hands. "You'll be happy to know your photos turned out perfectly."

James and I exchange a worried glance. "Photos?"

"Yes, your photos. You did spring for the commemorative package." The man motions us over to a pair of chairs. "You wait right here, and I'll be back with your things."

Once we're alone, I lean toward James. "You're going to want to watch him delete the originals before we get out of here."

"One step ahead of you." He fishes into his pocket for his wallet. I try not to gape at the wad of cash he pulls out.

It would seem the royal house of Rhodon is serious about keeping a lid on this.

I feel a twinge of guilt thinking about the story my editor will expect from me when I get back to New York. I am well aware of what he'll want. But given the situation, I don't feel entirely ethical handing James over.

The clerk returns with an oversized box. James's eyes go wide as he removes the lid and pulls out a gold-framed photograph. He tilts it my way.

"At least we look happy."

And completely blitzed. Really, you should have to take a Breathalyzer before you say I do. That said, in the picture we have our arms wrapped around each other and wide smiles on our faces. I am also looking at James like he is the most wonderful and fascinating person I have ever laid eyes on.

I really wish I could remember more of last night.

Handing me the box, James rises to his feet. "Sir, would you mind if we spoke in private?"

Surprise registers on the man's face, but he guides James to his office. While they're away, I look through the rest of the box. I paid for it, after all. I might as well look my fill before we toss it in the incinerator.

Mostly they're variations of the framed photo. Our faces on a coffee mug. On a decorative pillowcase. On a phone cover that won't fit either of our devices.

In one of the pictures, I'm slipping a ring on his finger. In another, his arms are around me. One hand cupping my ass, pulling me against him. My fingers are laced in his hair. And we're kissing with more tongue than should be allowed at a wedding ceremony.

Still, despite the sloppiness of it all, it looks fun. And, I have to admit, kind of hot.

By the time James and the manager return, I've made my way through the whole box. While it's tempting to keep one picture as a personal keepsake, I know it would be wrong. I may owe Ned and the magazine a royal story, but they are not getting this one.

I rise and follow James out the door. "Were you successful?"

He pats the pocket of his suit jacket. "I watched him delete the digital copies, and I have his signature swearing he won't sell us out."

I am curious how much that set him back. It is on the tip of my tongue to pry for details when I spot a photographer out of the corner of my eyes. A couple of the even sleazier publications always keep a couple of photogs in Vegas.

They're in place to capture any celebrities making walks of shame—or walks down the aisle.

This one has his lens focused on us.

"Photographer at two o'clock," I say.

James follows my direction and his eyes go wide before he holds up his hand to cover his face. "Shit."

"Come on." Shoving the box at him and grabbing him by the other hand, I lead him down an alleyway to a busy intersection.

Channeling my inner New Yorker, I flag down a cab and pull James into the backseat of it. In our hurry, he falls on top of me as we slam the door shut.

Our chests rise up and down, our faces inches from each other. I can't help but let my gaze wander to his lips. With his hard body pressed against me, I wonder what it would be like to kiss him.

Though I can't remember what it felt like last night, I have no doubt it would be un-freaking-believable.

I know it is a mistake, but I can't resist leaning forward. His mouth lowers toward mine. My eyes flutter shut, my heart pounding in anticipation.

Until the cab driver asks where we're headed.

Eyes open, I shove myself upright before my imagination and libido can get the better of me.

"Do you have that address for a lawyer?"

It takes him a moment to react, but at last, he nods and tells the driver where to go.

"Sorry about that." He leans back in his seat. "Reporters can be vultures."

FOUR

JAMES

Getting an annulment is surprisingly easy. The lawyer already had the necessary paperwork drawn up. We signed our names, and he shook our hands saying he would notify us as soon as the judge signed off on it.

They do everything fast here in Vegas. Breakfasts. Weddings. Break-ups.

As we step out of the lawyer's office, I cannot help but feel like I owe Alyssa some sort of explanation for our earlier run-in with the paparazzo. Taking her by the arm, I pull her into an alcove.

"You are probably curious about the photographer. And money." I glance down at myself. "And the suit."

She shakes her head. "We agreed on no history. No reality. I'm still good with that."

I eye her closely. "You are not the least bit curious?"

"Oh, sure, I am." Her full lips curve up and my breath

catches. What I wouldn't give to taste that sassy mouth of hers right now. "But we made a promise to each other."

That we did. Swallowing hard, I release my hold on her arm and take a step back. I shove my hands in my pocket.

"So what now?"

Alyssa leans against the building and stares at the ground. "I should probably get back to New York."

She does not sound entirely excited about that prospect. And neither do I, come to think of it. While I understand we will have to part ways at some point, the thought of saying our good-byes right now makes my stomach drop. Like I am behind the wheel of a car and there are no brakes.

But I can certainly put the brakes on facing reality for another day.

"What if you go back tomorrow."

Alyssa glances up at me. "How's that?"

"What if we stay here for the day? Have a little fun. Get to know each other."

She arches an eyebrow. "I thought we were planning on staying strangers."

"What if we amend the rules? No talk about our pasts. No talk about the future. We just live in the moment. Take each second as it comes."

Alyssa purses her lips in contemplation. I suddenly grow hard imagining those lips pressed against various parts of my body.

She has not said no yet. Which means there is still a chance at her saying yes. I sincerely hope she will say yes.

"I have never been to Las Vegas and after this, I doubt I will be back any time soon." I nudge her gently. "What do you say we spend one day having fun?"

"And when it is all over?"

I grin at her. "This only works if we promise not to talk about or think of the future."

Shaking her head, a grin spreads across those full, distracting lips of hers.

"I can't believe I'm agreeing to this, but what the hell. Let's do it."

ALYSSA

"Okay," I say, nearly out of breath from laughing while running the last block. "I can't keep going."

"Come on." James is almost as out of breath as I am. "I thought this was the city that doesn't sleep."

"That's New York."

His brows knit together. "What is Vegas then?"

"Sin City." I lean against a building and take a deep breath. "What happens here stays here."

"I like the sounds of that." He wiggles those thick eyebrows at me. "You cannot quit now. I still have one more turn to go."

After the whirlwind of an afternoon and evening we've had, I can barely stand upright on my two feet. Especially because those two feet are wearing a pair of heels so high, they should be illegal. Normally, I wouldn't wear anything like that. Then again, nothing about today has been normal.

And I'm not just talking about waking up in bed married to an honest-to-God prince, annulling an impulsive marriage, and dodging a photographer.

When James proposed we spend the day together, I had no idea where it would lead. We took turns picking out activities. Like last night, everything escalated quickly. Only this time, we said no to tequila and champagne.

A gentleman through and through, James insisted I go first in picking an activity. I started small by taking him to one of those wax museums filled with replicas of celebrities. Next, he showed off by taking me on a helicopter tour of the city and Hoover Dam. We followed that with my choice of indoor skydiving. Once our stomachs were settled, he took me out for sushi at a restaurant I could never afford on my own. So I maxed out my personal credit card and bought tickets to a show.

James was a good sport about it—even though most of the show included well-formed men stripping.

Through it all, we laughed and somehow managed to swap stories about our lives without giving details about our true identities. I almost feel guilty about knowing his. Though, the more time I spend with him, the less he seems like a playboy prince with a reputation that could make you blush. He's just James. And James is a lot of fun.

And unbelievably sexy in that suit of his.

We were so giddy from laughing after the show, we practically raced back to our hotel. Now I am wiped. But, as James pointed out, it is his turn to pick an activity. I can't be a spoilsport now.

"Okay." I push away from the building, accepting the offer of his arm to lean on. "One more shenanigan. Then it's time for bed."

"Shenanigan," he repeats. The word sounds ridiculous coming from that posh mouth of his. A posh mouth that I imagine is fully capable of doing not-so-posh things to a woman's body.

Guiding me through the doors of our hotel, James leans forward and whispers something to one of the concierges. A moment later, a man in an impeccably tailored black suit steps forward.

"If you will follow me, Mr. and Mrs. James."

I arch an eyebrow, and James covers my hand on his arm. "Just go with it."

Taking small steps forward on my aching feet, we're led through the doors into the casino. My heart sinks for a moment. Gambling. It really isn't my thing. I went to Atlantic City once with some friends. I spent the whole time mentally calculating all of the money we lost at the tables. After twenty bucks, I couldn't take it anymore and spent the rest of the weekend reading by the pool.

Still, this is James's turn. If he wants to throw away Rhodon's treasury on cards. It would make a great story for the magazine. Of course, I could never bring myself to write it.

The more time I spend with James, the more I realize I won't be able to report anything back to my boss. I know it's my job, but I just can't. I can't betray James and the crazy, exhilarating twenty-four hours we've shared.

And I'll just have to face the consequences. Even if that means moving back home to live with my parents.

We move past the tables and through a curtained area. Behind it, we pass a row of doors. The suit-wearing man knocks three times, and it swings open.

The man gives a bow of sorts and steps away.

I glance up at James. "What's this?"

"For the next hour, it's our private gambling room. We can set our own stakes and play whatever we want."

Okay, I have to admit, that sounds kind of fun.

"What if I say I want to play Go Fish?"

James lifts his shoulder. "Then I can dismiss the dealer, and we can play Go Fish until they kick us out."

I can't help but giggle at the thought of playing Go Fish in a private room at a casino. It's too ridiculous to pass up.

"What do you say?" James asks.
"I say go fish."

FIVE

JAMES

Barely ten minutes into our game of Go Fish, Alyssa tosses her cards down on the table.

"Okay, I'm sorry." She shakes her head in frustration. "This isn't very fun, is it."

"I am having a good time."

She narrows her eyes at me. "Be honest. This game loses its intrigue when you're an adult."

I pull a face and she points a finger at me. "Ha! I knew it. You were just being a gentleman. You are bored out of your mind."

"Fine." I throw up my hands. "I was being polite. But you are correct. The game does not have the same thrill as Texas hold-em."

"You're missing the thrill of the bet?"

"Something like that."

Alyssa opens her mouth to say something than shakes her head. My curiosity is piqued.

"What?" I ask when she shows no signs of speaking.

"No, it's ridiculous."

"I like ridiculous things."

"You would." She grins. "Fine. It's totally something high school or college kids would do, but . . . we could play strip Go Fish."

I am most definitely interested in seeing where this goes.

I feign an interest in something on my tie. "I would be up for giving it a shot."

"Of course you would." Alyssa rolls her eyes, which oddly enough makes me want to kiss her. "You're a man and you're wearing at least twice as much clothing as I am right now."

"I would be willing to level the playing field." To show her my sincerity, I remove my coat, belt, and shoes. "Now we each have six pieces to go."

Laughing, Alyssa leans forward. "Deal me in."

The first few turns, each of us has one of the cards the other needs. I am about to suggest we switch to poker when Alyssa asks if I have in threes.

"I do not." I arch an eyebrow at her. "Go fish."

Grinning good-naturedly, Alyssa kicks off one of her high-heeled shoes and reaches for a card in the middle of the table. "Your turn."

"Got any deuces?"

She shakes her head. "Go fish."

Eyebrows raised, I remove my tie and toss it to her.

Her other shoe goes next. Then both of my socks. Then my shirt. I will admit to taking a little extra care as I undo one button after the other.

And, if I am not mistaken, the glisten of interest in her eye belongs entirely to me.

I am rewarded a minute later when she stands up and

slowly wriggles out of her pants. My eyes hungrily feast on the smooth skin below her T-shirt, and the hint of black lace panties beneath it.

"Got any deuces?"

She grins. "You know I don't."

I tug off my own pants before she can say "go fish."

Biting down on her lips. She asks if I have threes, again.

I shake my head. As she reaches for the bottom of her shirt, I reach across the table.

"Allow me."

She freezes, watching me carefully as I rise and step around the table. I pull her to her feet, easing the top up her waist, my thumbs stroking her skin, as I toss it over her head.

Now it is just the two of us. Her in a black bra and panty set. Me in my boxer briefs, harder then I've ever been before. I cannot resist the temptation any longer.

"Alyssa?"

"Hmm?"

I stroke a finger over her lips. They part and her tongue dips out to stroke it.

My control breaks. My mouth crashes onto hers, hungry like a man who hasn't had food or water in days. Her hands slide up my bare back, gripping onto the muscles of my shoulders, pulling me even closer.

Our tongues clash and our breaths gasp. One of my hands travels down her waist and slides into her panties.

Dear, God. She is so wet.

Swiping the cards and chips to the floor with one swift motion, I lift Alyssa to the table. My fingers dive into her hair, tugging her head back, exposing her neck. My mouth explores as she gasps.

Gliding up over her, my hard cock presses against her, only the thin barrier of fabric between us.

If I ripped them off, I could make her mine right now.

As I think about driving into her, I am aware of the busy Vegas casino just outside the door. While I would love nothing more than to make her come over and over—to bury myself deep inside of her—I do not want to risk the chance of someone walking in on us.

I want to be the only one who sees her fall over the edge of pleasure.

Pulling back, I gaze down at her, unable to resist caressing her cheek with my knuckles.

"Let me have you?"

She nods.

"But not here. I want you loud when I take you."

ALYSSA

We're in our room and naked again in under five minutes. Which has to be a world record.

But right now I am not interested in world records. Not when I want to get my hands all over James's well-formed body.

Not when I need him to touch every inch of my own.

Eyeing me hungrily, James pulls me to the bed. Once I'm seated, he pushes me down so I am flat on my back. I push up on my elbows in time to watch him kneel between my legs.

His dark eyes meet my gaze as he scrapes the stubble of his day-old beard along my inner thigh. My fingers dig into the bedspread.

He lifts his head again. "I want to make you scream before I fuck you. Don't be shy about telling me what you like."

Though I've never been loud in bed before, I nod in agreement.

He gives me a hot, opened-mouthed kiss on my navel in approval. His tongue trails a path down around my bush, leaving goosebumps and tingles in its wake. He presses slow, wet kisses along my thigh as one of his long fingers parts my pussy to find my clit.

His thumb moves around it slowly, sending an instant jolt of pleasure through me.

I cry out.

"You like that?"

I nod. "Yes."

"How about this?"

Continuing to move his thumb around my nub, he slides a finger inside of me.

I let out another sound, one I've never heard before.

He chuckles. "I will take that as a 'yes, please.'"

"Yes, please." And then I come completely undone as his mouth replaces his thumb and he slides two more fingers inside of me. Stroking my wall. Finding the g-spot that has eluded all of my past boyfriends.

The pleasure builds and grows inside of me as he inserts another finger. I gasp, gripping the comforter, holding on for dear life, as I go over the edge and the orgasm radiates through me.

I call out his name and God's, and he stays with me, prolonging the pleasure until all that exists in this world is James and me and what he is doing to my body.

While I draw deep breaths, I am vaguely aware of James rising to his feet. A moment later, he rips open the foil of a condom. I lean up again watching as he glides it on with expertise.

Pulling me to my feet, James leads me to the window

overlooking the city and the lights below us. Kissing my neck with his full lips, still glistening from me, he pulls away. Before I can react, he braces my hands on the back of the chair. He lifts one of my legs, so I'm partially kneeling on it. His palms move over me, cupping my breast, and fingering me again. While I look down at the city, he enters me in one swift motion.

I cry out, reaching my hand over my shoulder to grab his hair.

He thrusts in and out, faster, harder, with a skill I've never experienced before. The fronts of his thighs press against the backs of mine.

As my insides begin to quake again, I hear James's breaths quicken. He rides me, pushing us both toward the peak of Everest.

And when I find it again, I cry out. He groans as he thrusts into me one more time, my orgasm pushing us both over.

His hands cover mine, gripping onto the back of the chair to keep us upright while our breaths and heartbeats steady.

That was like nothing I have ever felt before. And somewhere inside of me, I know it is like nothing I will ever experience again without him.

Seconds, maybe minutes later, James slides out of me. He carries me back to the bed like it is no effort. When we are settled between the covers, my head on his chest and his arms wrapped around me, he presses a kiss to my forehead.

"There's something I want to tell you."

Then, with our fingers laced together, James tells me he's a prince. He tells me about his childhood, growing up the youngest child of a strict king. He tells me about earning a bad boy reputation that is only half merited. He tells me about finding his place at school and with numbers.

Because they made sense and made him feel like a normal person.

On and on.

I listen in silence, falling deeper and deeper in love with him.

I have to tell him my truth as well. But he dozes off in the middle of his story, leaving me to think about it in silence. I will tell him everything first thing in the morning. And I hope he doesn't hate me once he knows.

SIX

JAMES

I nuzzle Alyssa awake. Though I could watch her sleep for hours, I know she has a plane ticket back to New York later this morning. My stomach twists at that thought. Though we promised to enjoy only the moment, I will be damned if I let her walk out of my life never to be seen again.

What happened between us was more than sex. Surely she must see that. The way we connected, both in and out of bed, is something else. Something I do not think we can walk away from and forget.

Yawning, Alyssa rubs her eyes and looks up at me. "How is it possible?"

I frown. "What?"

"You look even more handsome in the morning." She reaches up to run one hand through my disheveled hair and the other over my stubble. I am not sure my father would approve of either, but I like that she does. "I look like a troll."

"Hey, that is my wife you are talking about."

"Your soon to be ex-wife."

Her words make my heart hitch, even though I know they are true. I dismiss the feeling. We can talk about the future later.

But first things first. "You are my wife at this very moment. We might as well make the most of it."

I dive under the covers, and a moment later she is giggling. God, I love that sound. It makes me ravenous and hard. I am about to take care of both of those issues when there is a pounding at the hotel door.

I pop out from under the blanket. "We're good on towels, thanks."

Alyssa covers her mouth to stifle a laugh.

"Open the damn door, James."

I freeze.

Alyssa eyes me cautiously. "Who is that?"

"That would be my big brother." I bolt up, pulling on my boxer briefs and handing her a robe. "I know we said no strings, but I am afraid that is about to change, my dear."

"Wait," she calls out as she pulls on her robe. "There's something I should tell you first."

"We can discuss it after I send my brother packing."

"No, please, I—"

I open the door to find an annoyed-looking Henry on the other side.

"You are lucky Father did not send his guards."

I wince. "So Dad knows?"

"Dad knows everything. Probably more than you do." Henry looks behind me to where Alyssa has now pulled on the robe but is still hanging out in the background. "You, I imagine, are Alyssa Giles?"

"I am." Her voice shakes.

I turn in concern. "Do not worry. Henry is harmless."

Alyssa shakes her head. "No, he is not."

"I am afraid your blushing bride is correct." Henry steps inside and closes the door behind him. "As I said, our father knows more than you can imagine."

"Please." Alyssa steps toward Henry. "I know I have no reason for you to do anything I ask, but let me tell him."

My heart freezes, pumping ice through my veins. "Tell me what?"

She runs a hand through her messy blonde hair and takes a shaky breath. "Our meeting wasn't an accident. I work for a magazine."

"What magazine?"

She gives the name of one of the more sordid publications littering the grocery stores and the Internet.

"I'm a researcher there." Her gaze moves to the hideous burnt mustard carpeting. "I was supposed to look for a fresh and unique angle to pass on to one of the reporters on our staff."

"So you knew who I was the whole time?" My frozen heart rips into shreds.

She nods. "But I swear, I didn't plan on any of this happening. And I haven't sent so much as a picture back to my boss."

I wish I could believe her. "You will have to forgive me if I do not take your word for it."

"I don't have any record of anything." She offers me her phone. "Take a look. I promise you'll find it's clean."

My jaw ticks and I turn my gaze out the window. I can still see them in the reflection.

"If you do that is your business." I swallow hard against a lump in my throat. "Take your fifteen minutes of fame. What do I care?"

Sighing, Henry steps forward. "If it is all the same to you, I would like to check."

"Please. Do." She practically shoves it at him.

I continue to stare blankly out the window wondering how I could ever be so foolish. A few minutes later, Henry hands Alyssa back the phone.

"I am by no means a cybersecurity expert, but it looks clean."

His expression seems to soften as he watches Alyssa with more interest.

"Has it hit the news yet?" I ask.

Henry shakes his head still looking at her. "But the palace just had a call from a publication."

"Hers?"

"Another one. But we figure it is only a matter of time."

Nodding, I spare a glance at Alyssa who is giving Meryl Streep a run for her money with her ability to look distraught.

"I think you have a flight to catch."

"James please." She clutches her hands together at her chest. The anguish in her voice is another dagger through my chest. "I can explain. What happened between us is real. I wanted to tell you. I love you. I should have—"

"Stop." My jaw ticks. "Whatever we did or did not have is over."

With that, I excuse myself and lock the bathroom door behind me. I stare into the mirror wondering how I could possibly have been so stupid.

SEVEN

ALYSSA

I'm so numb on the trip from Las Vegas to New York, I barely notice when the airport shuttle driver pulls up in front of my apartment. He clears his throat twice before I even realize we've arrived.

Inside, I set my tote bag and purse on my coffee table and sink into my couch. Mr. Darcy, my black and white tuxedo cat, sprints across the room to let me know what he thinks about my impulsively leaving him alone for forty-eight hours. But his whines quickly turn into mews as he hops on my lap to rub his face with mine.

He's a little love. And, it seems, unlike some princes I know, he can forgive and forget.

Tears roll down my cheeks only earning me even more snuggles and affection from Mr. Darcy. Thank goodness he isn't like his namesake. If he was, he would be listing off all of the ways I've screwed up my life in the past couple of days—heck, years.

I'm full-fledged open-mouthed ugly crying when my phone rings. I freeze mid-sob and reach into my purse. Did James have a change of heart? Is he going to forgive me? Hope brews until I get my hands on the phone and read the display.

It's Ned.

Of course. Who else could it be?

I'd have to be an idiot to think James could forgive me after what I did. Unfortunately, as I've proven over and over, I am an idiot.

Sighing, I answer the phone. He doesn't bother with any niceties.

"When you said you had one hell of an inside angle, I'll admit, I never expected this."

Yeah, neither did I.

"I only wish you would've told us before we got scooped," he adds. "So, when can I expect your notes."

"I'm not sure it would be appropriate given everything that's happened," I say lamely. I have been so stupid. If I had the energy, I'd slap myself to see if it would help knock sense into me.

"What are you saying?"

I take a deep breath. "I'm not giving you anything."

"Wait a minute." I can practically see Ned's face turning red on the other end of the line. "Let me see if I've got this straight. You've spent most of the past forty-eight hours with the playboy prince of Rhodon."

"Correct." Though, I never so much as saw him glance at another woman when we were together. And he had ample opportunity.

"You used company funds to book yourself travel."

"Which I've already reimbursed." True to his word, James had paid me back for everything.

Ned sighs. "You married the guy."

"Briefly."

"And you aren't going to give us anything."

"I didn't marry him to get a story."

"Then why did you?"

That's the question I've been trying to answer for the past couple of days, isn't it? "Honestly, and this is off the record. But I don't know why I married him."

"You don't?"

"I was drunker than any human has probably been in the history of drunken nights." But it wasn't just an alcohol-infused mistake. I see that now. "Plus, I like him."

It's more than that. Somehow, in the whirlwind of everything, I fell for James.

The line goes silent, and I hold my breath waiting for Ned's response. Honestly, I'll be surprised if the next words out of his mouth don't include my being fired.

"That's the problem, isn't it?" he asks at last. "You started to see the prince as a human and not the subject of your article."

"He is human. All of the people in our articles are."

"You can't look at them that way in this industry. Not if you want to make a career out of it."

"But I don't want to make this a career." Now that the words are out of my mouth, some small weight lifts from my shoulders. "This was only supposed to be a temporary job. Something I did to break into journalism."

"And now it's done."

"Well, if that's how you feel . . ."

We hang up a moment later after Ned tells me I'll need to pick up my things from the office and that I may be hearing from their lawyers. But he never raises his voice. I guess he's better at accepting that something is over than I am.

I don't know how long I have been sitting there silently petting Mr. Darcy when my phone buzzes with an email. It's from the lawyer in Las Vegas. The judge signed the papers. Our marriage is officially null and void.

Just like my life and any hopes I have for happiness.

JAMES

The next day, Henry and I board our private jet to head home. For the first time in my life, I cannot wait to be back in Rhodon. I deserve the lecture that is sure to come from my father.

I slouch in my seat and stare gloomily at the tarmac.

"You're making headlines in the papers," Henry says from across the aisle.

I grunt in response.

"Everywhere I look, I see your ugly mug next to that beautiful woman's face."

"She was a mistake. One I will not make again." Monogamy does not suit me. Though the thought of going back to my libertine ways does not particularly thrill me either. Hell, I suppose it will just have to be celibacy. "Maybe I will become a priest."

Henry snorts. "I do not see that working out for you."

"It might be worth a shot." I pull the shutter down on the window, no longer interested in the world around me. "We both know I am rubbish with women."

"True. You might be a genius at numbers, but you are a fool with women." Henry shakes his head. "You always have been. Looks like you always will unless . . ."

"Unless what?"

"Unless you open your damn eyes to the woman you already have."

"You mean a reporter who pretended to be into me to get a story."

"What story?" He waves a pile of newspapers at me. He picks up the first. "'Ms. Giles could not be reached for comment.'" He chucks it aside and holds up the next. "'Sources say Giles is no longer working for the magazine.'" He tosses that away and reads on and on.

Every article in every publication is the same. Alyssa is not talking. She either quit her job or was fired. No one has seen her, even though reporters are parked outside every exit of her building.

"You are flying home in a private jet and pouting," Henry says throwing aside the last article. "Your wife gave up her job and every lucrative offer to sell her story. She is a prisoner in her own home. Her life is forever changed."

So is mine. Even if it may not look like it to the world or my brother. "She's not my wife. The annulment went through."

Henry's fist comes down on his tray table, knocking a bottle of water over. "You know what I damn well mean. You are acting like you are the only one coming out of this experience damaged."

"She lied to me."

Some of the fury eases from Henry's face. "I know, little brother. You have every right to be upset. But didn't you say you had an agreement? No questions about your real lives."

I shrug. "She knew who I was the whole time."

"Yet she did not ask you for any family secrets, or did she?"

Come to think of it . . . no. She did not. And she had plenty of opportunities."

"Any questions about our sister's pregnancy or husband?"

I shake my head.

"Anything about Alex and his girlfriend? Or about Father's health? Or about the change in the country's line of succession?"

"She asked nothing."

"Either she is a terrible journalist, or she was holding up her end of the bargain." Henry arches an eyebrow. "Don't you think it might be worth figuring out?"

My mind races with dozens of questions and thoughts. They all come back to one thing. In the time I was with Alyssa, I felt happy and whole. In the time we have been apart, I have been miserable.

"She is the only woman I have been with who never called me your highness," I say at last. "She spoke to me like I was a real man. Not a prince."

"Either she is destined to win an Oscar, or you have found yourself a keeper. I saw the way she looked at you." Henry pulls up a photo on his phone and hands it to me. "You look pretty happy here."

There, on the screen, is a picture of Alyssa and I walking hand in hand through Vegas. It is not from our drunken first night together, but a security image from our marathon adventure the following day. We have giant grins on our faces. She is looking at me like I matter. Not as her meal ticket. Not as a story. Just as the man she wants to be with.

And I am looking at her like she is everything.

Am I willing to walk away from that just because our beginning was a little touch and go? There is only one way to find out.

Sitting up in my seat, I straighten my tie. "Do you think we could make a slight change in our flight plan?"

Henry grins. "I already made it."

EIGHT

ALYSSA

If the reporters don't clear out in the next twenty-four hours, I may starve to death.

Okay, I probably won't die that soon. But I am down to my last box of macaroni and cheese. I don't even have milk or butter for fixing it up.

A couple of my friends have offered to bring me supplies, but I can't ask them to face the media. Worse, I'm not entirely sure I can trust them. Most of my friends work for some news outlet or another. I can't be sure they won't go back to their own editors and report that the former Mrs. Prince James hasn't washed her hair and has holes in her leggings.

I contemplated food delivery, but after three reporters already tried posing as couriers, I'm not willing to risk it.

Fortunately, Mr. Darcy has enough food to last him for another week, or I might end up murdered in my bed.

That is if I could close my eyes long enough to sleep.

Every time I try, visions of James fill my head. Then the questions start.

Would things have turned out differently if I'd told him who I was from the start?

Was there ever a chance for us?

What am I going to do now that I'm out of a job, and I have nothing but true crime documentaries on Netflix?

How am I going to pay for Netflix?

At some point, I'm going to have to leave this apartment. I'm going to have to get groceries. I'm going to have to get a new job. I'm going to have to get a life.

But right now, I'm not even sure where to begin.

So I just keep hitting "next episode" when one episode of a grizzly murder show ends. I'm doing just that when there's a knock at my door.

"Go away!" I shout from my position curled up on my couch.

The knocking turns into pounding.

"I said get out of here. I'll call the cops."

I'm sure they'll be here to help just as soon as they finish solving all of their cases, like the one playing out on the TV right now.

Bang. Bang. Bang.

Okay. That's enough. How is a person supposed to solve a cold case from the comfort of her sofa with that ruckus? I throw open the door, fully prepared to give this journalist the "no comment" of a lifetime, but freeze.

There looking impeccably handsome and put together in a blue suit, is James. My heart somehow sinks and soars in one instance.

"May I come in?" He glances over his shoulder. "This place is crawling with reporters."

Yeah, no kidding. I hold the door open wider and step

aside. I tug my oversized sweater around my body more tightly and run my fingers through my hair like that's somehow going to help me look like less of a mess.

James glances around my studio apartment. He doesn't give away any impression of his thoughts. Mr. Darcy hops down from his post and races over to run figure eights between James's legs.

Grinning, he lowers to give my cat a scratch under his chin. "You didn't mention you had a kid."

I bite back a smile of my own. Does he really think he can just stroll in here as if nothing happened?

"I didn't think it mattered, what with you telling me to get out of your life."

He winces and pushes himself back to his feet. "You're right. I over-reacted."

The thing is. He didn't.

"If the roles had been reversed, I'm sure I would have done the same." I gesture to the couch. "Would you like to sit?"

"In a minute." James moves toward me. "I tried working out exactly what to say on the flight here. It did not go well. You are a writer. A good one at that."

"How could you possibly know? I only published a few pieces with that trashy magazine."

"I found some of your work from college online."

He searched out my old college clips? I chew on the inside of my cheek, not sure how to feel about that. Having hope seems dangerous right now.

"Well, what did you come up with?"

"Nothing good." He lifts a shoulder. "Try as I might, I could not find the perfect words to tell you how sorry I am. To tell you that running away with you was the best decision

I ever made. To say I want us to get to know each other's real lives and to be part of them."

He raises a hand to my cheek. "Mostly, I want to ask if you could possibly give me another chance. And to say I already love you more than you will ever know."

A tear slips from my eye, and he wipes it with his thumb.

I swallow, trying to hold back more tears. "That was pretty good."

"For a first try." He lifts my chin and lowers his mouth until it is a breath away from mine. "But if you are game, I would like to make it all up to you."

"I'm a big believer in second chances."

He arches an eyebrow. "Are you?"

"I am now."

EPILOGUE

ALYSSA

six months later

As I check the contents of my suitcase against my checklist for the fifth time, I give James a worried look as he steps into the bedroom of our flat in Oxford.

"On a scale of one to ten, what are the odds your father has a firing squad waiting to take me away when we get there?"

"Rhodon outlawed the death penalty more than fifty years ago."

At least I don't have to write a will. I cross that off of my to-do list.

"Well, what are the odds he has me hauled me off to the dungeon?"

"My great grandfather converted the dungeons into an extra kitchen and servants quarters before the war."

"Oh." I hadn't realized the royal family of Rhodon was quite so progressive.

James drops onto the bed and Mr. Darcy hops up next to him. He rubs his face against James's palm. My cat has fallen just as hard for James as I did.

We both made the move to England about four months ago. James has another six months to go on his appointment with the university. I'm using the time to write the book I've always wanted. It's about an American girl who falls in love with a prince and moves halfway around the world to live happily ever after with him.

It's all fiction, of course. But when I publish, I'll use a pen name. After the firestorm we caused with our quickie marriage and annulment, the last thing I want to do is create more fodder for the media.

Or give the royals more reason to hate me.

"Are you sure I should go with you?" I ask. "I only met your sister one time. While I'm happy for her and Ryan, I just don't see how much help I'll be at a baptism."

Sighing, James reaches out for me. Setting aside my notebook and pen, I take his hands.

"You don't need to worry about my family." He raises our linked hands to his lips. His dark gaze turns sultry. "Besides, my love, my family is your family now."

He means that quite literally. Last week, at the end of our holiday in Spain, we found ourselves in Gibraltar. As the Las Vegas of Europe, we ended up before a judge promising to love and honor each other until death do we part. Only this time we were both completely sober and intend to keep our vows.

"Your father is going to freak out."

"Probably." James chuckles and holds on tighter to my hands as I try to pull away. "But you're in luck. Dad always had a soft spot for me."

"You really have led a charmed life."

"I won't deny it." He kisses my hands once more and releases them. "You and your love will always be proof of that."

HENRY

RIDICULOUSLY ROYAL #4

ONE

HENRY

The front doors of the palace swing open. I am barely out of the silver Maserati when my sister throws herself at me. I just have time to raise my arms around Princess Sarah of Rhodon as the force of her hug throws against my car.

"You would think I have just come back from war or an expedition to Mars." I chuckle but pull her in tighter. "It has only been a few months."

"Three months, six days, and nine and a half hours."

"Not that you are counting."

"I had my secretary check. I was sure it had been even longer."

I pull back so I can tease her. But as I catch a proper glimpse of her face, my heart lurches. Eighteen months ago, my twin sister was a picture of health. Glowing skin from regular spa dates, a quick bright smile that could lighten anyone's mood, and a pair of brown eyes that always seemed to sparkle like she had a secret.

Now, I can see she has been made up carefully to cover dark circles under her eyes. Her cheeks sink in. And the light in her expression seems to be all but extinguished.

"Hey." I give her a one-armed squeeze. "You alright?"

She forces her lips into a smile. "I am wonderful. I should be asking you, Mr. Jetsetter."

"The life of a traveling prince does have its perks." Though, in truth, I miss being able to stay put for longer than eight weeks at a time.

Our lives have all been turned upside down during the past eighteen months. That was when we learned that government officials and doctors had conspired to say I—and not my sister—was the firstborn twin.

Sarah became the new heir-apparent. Our father threw her into appointments and tutoring sessions to cram twenty-five years of education into one. All while falling in love with her bodyguard, getting married, and giving birth to the future queen of Rhodon.

Our brother Alex briefly returned to the military but has become an official "working" member of the family since he married a celebrity baker last month.

James is finishing his research fellowship in Economics at Oxford with his reporter ex-wife-turned-live-in-girlfriend.

And I am living out of a suitcase to be out of sight and out of mind. Our father, the king, claims I can best serve the country as a goodwill ambassador making private visits to our friends and colleagues around the world.

We all know better. We all know he wants me away so the people of Rhodon can forget I even exist.

"I hate that father has done this to you," Sarah says, her lips curving back down. "Ryan and I have repeatedly told him your exile is only making matters worse."

"I am sure father loved being told what to do by you."

She lifts a shoulder. "I don't care. I need you, Henry."

"I am here." A camera flashes. Frowning at the paparazzo, I slip an arm around her shoulders and guide her into the palace. "And I am eager to see my goddaughter again."

"Your niece will be thrilled to see you too."

"Three-month-old babies can talk, can they?"

Sarah elbows me in the ribs. "Well, I am thrilled to have Cat see you. When it came time to pick her godparents, I knew there could be no one but you."

"And how did father take that proclamation?"

She stills, but I already know. Even if our father had not felt it necessary to send me a note on the subject, I would have known. It is the king's opinion that the role of godfather is far too attention-grabbing and news-worthy. He would rather that I slip in and out of the baptism as a guest without being photographed.

"Father may control most of my life now," Sarah says. "But I have the final say on what is best for my family."

"Just not what is best for you." I grip onto her tighter before she can pull away. "Sarah, you never need to pretend with me. I can see what he is doing to you."

A tear slips down her cheek, and she swipes away at hit so quickly, I almost miss it.

"Father is still unconvinced the people have accepted me as the future queen. He says it might have been easier if Catherine had been a boy."

Fury slices through me. "That kind of backward thinking has no place in our country's present or future."

"No, but it is my job to do what I can to win the naysayers over." She gives me a weak grin. "I took off two weeks after delivery, and I have been back at full duties since."

The anger turns to sadness, as I can sense my sister's guilt and pain like they are my very own.

"Is it necessary?"

"This is unchartered territory." She lifts a shoulder and seems to choose her next words carefully. "I feel . . . torn between serving our country and being the wife and mother Ryan and Catherine deserve. I spend my days running between meetings, ribbon cuttings, and classes. All while pumping in the car in between. At night I stay up with my daughter. I would never see Ryan if he was not part of my security detail."

"And you are running yourself ragged in the process."

"It is only temporary."

"Temporary or not, you deserve a nap."

The word nap puts a hint of that familiar sparkle in her eye for a second. "I was planning on spending a few minutes with Catherine after this next meeting. Her nap is almost over."

"How about I go and spend some one-on-one time with my niece while you get some much-needed rest."

Sarah purses her lips. "She still has about forty-five minutes left in her nap."

"I can get in a quick workout and shower first."

Her lips quiver a second before she presses them to my cheek, her arms wrapped around my waist again.

"I cannot tell you how good it is to have you home."

Then we part ways so she can go to her next meeting, and I can continue my life of idleness. I wish I could do more for her. Maybe I can convince Father . . . I shake that thought out of my head. No, it will take a lot more than pestering from his children to get the King of Rhodon to change his stubborn mind.

Country will always come first for the king.

TWO

LAUREN

Putting the baby down for a nap was harrowing to say the least.

Not that Catherine isn't the sweetest baby in the world. And nannying for her is a total dream. But when that little girl puts her mind to something, she accomplishes it. And when that mind is absolutely determined not to take a nap—even though she can barely keep her eyes open—she doesn't mess around.

If she's already this dedicated and focused at three months old, I can only imagine what she'll be like when she's queen.

Not that I'll really see much of that. I'm only in Rhodon for the summer while my grandmother—the official palace nanny—recovers from knee replacement surgery.

Armed with the baby monitor, I slip into my bedroom, which is next to hers. The princess encourages me to use nap time to work on summer school courses. I'm halfway through my master's degree in early childhood education. Taking a couple of classes this summer will give me a leg up when I'm back in the fall.

I'm barely through the door when I catch a movement in the corner of the room. Whipping around to investigate, I let out a scream that is quickly silenced by a strong hand. I am pulled against a solid, muscular chest of a man at least six inches taller than me.

"My family has had journalists go to extreme lengths to get an exclusive story on the royal family," the deep voice says. "But I can say I have never seen someone sneak into my bedroom."

His bedroom? That has to be the lamest excuse for a fake story I've ever heard. I struggle against his hold without luck.

Out of options, I take the only one left. I step down hard on one of his feet, shove an elbow to his gut, and finish with a fist to the groin.

As he keels over in pain, I jump away. I reach for my phone ready to call Catherine's father. Not only is he a duke, but he works for palace security. He'll have this guy in a dungeon in five minutes.

I nearly push send when the would-be assailant's groan catches my attention. He rolls over, and I finally get a glimpse of his face.

And I nearly lose my breath.

"Oh, shit." Unless I'm mistaken, I've just punched Prince Henry of Rhodon in the nuts. "Please tell me you're Henry."

"Who the hell else would I be?" He glares up at me. "I might ask who you are and what you are doing in my room."

"But this is my room." My eyes widen. "Wait. I just remembered. The princess gave me your old room so I'd be closer to the nursery. Your new room is down the hall."

"She didn't say anything."

"She's a new mom working more than full-time hours. I'd say she has good reason to be forgetful."

Henry lets out an expletive as he pushes himself up to his feet. Once he reaches his full height, and his glare is directed straight at me, my heart skips a beat.

The cheatsheet my grandma gave me to study did not do this man justice. In those pictures, he was handsome. In person, it's a wonder my panties haven't completely melted away.

I almost glance down to check to make sure they're still there but catch myself in time.

Besides, I can't quite bring myself to look away from those intense green eyes that are focused on my face.

"I am still waiting," he says.

"For what?"

"For you to tell me just who the hell you are and why you are sleeping in my bed."

The thought of actually sharing the same bed with him is enough to make my cheeks flush bright red.

"I'm Lauren. I'm the nanny."

He snorts. "You are at least forty years too young to be Nanny Nora."

"She's my grandmother. Seriously," I add when he looks like he doesn't believe me. "My mom is her daughter. We live in Idaho."

"Nanny Nora has family in Idaho?"

I nod.

"Who knew?" Henry grins then, and I almost go into cardiac arrest right there.

These princes should come with warning labels. Something like "Do not stare directly into their faces or risk being blinded." Or at least super aroused.

Which is the very last thing I should be feeling just minutes after nearly removing his family jewels.

"Sorry about before." I pull a face. "I thought you might be here to kidnap me."

His face grows concerned. "Is there much danger of kidnapping?"

"Not at all. I just have an overactive imagination."

"It must run in the family." The frown eases from his face. "I remember your grandmother could spin quite a yarn."

"She tells the best stories."

And while she occasionally spilled a little tea about the royal family of Rhodon, she kept most of it to herself. She's a very good and reliable employee. It's no wonder the princess wanted her back.

Henry shoves his hands into the pockets of his sweatpants. "How long have you been here?"

"About three weeks."

"How long will you be staying?"

"Through the end of summer."

"What will you do after your time here is done?"

I feel like I'm in the middle of a pop quiz on the first day of a class I've never attended. Down to the little jolt of panic in my chest.

"I'll go back to grad school. In America."

He arches an eyebrow, and I don't know what to make of that. A lock of brown hair falls over his forehead giving him a rakish look. That makes me want to jump him.

Which would be bad. Very, very bad.

"Well, Lauren, it has been interesting meeting you." He grins as my face flushes red again. "I suppose I will see you around."

Then he slips out the door. The moment it latches

behind him, I rush to the window and throw it open. I gasp at the fresh air. Like it'll help.

For as long as I live, I will never forget those green eyes. Or how firm the prince's chest felt against my back.

THREE

HENRY

I toss and turn most of the night. Every time I close my eyes, all I can see is a pair of lips I would like to taste, a round ass I'd like to sink my fingers into, and breasts I'd like to nibble on.

Not to mention the pair of hazel eyes with specs of gold in them and the long mane of dark hair, perfect for gripping onto while sinking myself into her over and over.

I spent most of the night rock hard. After a failed cold shower, I had to jerk myself off. All the while imagining it was those lips on my cock and not my hand. If my sister knew I was having those kinds of thoughts about the nanny, she would toss me out of the palace now.

I skipped out on breakfast with the family and went for a run to work off some of the restless energy. When that did not do the trick, I took another shower. I tried reading a book. I even walked in the palace gardens.

None of it did a damn thing to get that beautiful vixen out of my mind.

Which is the only explanation I have for why I am now standing at the door to the nursery. I knock.

A moment later, Lauren appears with a baby against her shoulder. My cock twitches and my tongue nearly rolls out of my mouth. Even with spit-up dribbling down one shoulder, she is more stunning than I remember.

Her eyes widen? "What are you doing here?"

I grin. Thank goodness for clueless Americans. If the nanny were a Rhodinian, she would be falling all over herself to curtsy. Instead, she is giving me attitude.

I like the attitude.

"I wanted to get in a little face-time with my niece. I am her godfather, after all."

Which is not a lie. In all the excitement of the missed rooms yesterday, I did not have a chance to spend more than a passing moment with my niece.

Getting a chance to look her over is a bonus.

Sighing, Lauren pulls the door open wider and gestures for me to walk inside.

"I could actually use another pair of hands."

She holds Catherine out toward me, and I freeze.

"Oh, I am not sure I should hold her."

"Why not?"

"I . . ." How am I, a grown man, supposed to admit I am afraid of doing it wrong? "I have not been around a lot of babies."

She nods in understanding and guides me toward a rocking chair. "Sit."

I do as ordered. Then, she pulls a crescent-shaped pillow out and sets it on my lap.

"Hold your hands like this."

Again, I follow directions. Nodding in approval, she places the baby in my arms. She's so . . . tiny. Catherine's eyelids flutter open, and she smiles up at me. My heart melts. At this moment I know. If anyone tries to hurt my niece, I will kill them.

Grinning, I look at Lauren, who is watching us closely. "You're good at all of this."

"I'm not sure everyone agrees." She takes a seat next to me. Leaning over, she rearranges the blanket around Catherine. Her hand brushes against mine, sending a jolt of electricity through me.

"Who?"

"The king for one. I'm told he wasn't super stoked your sister hired me. Even with my grandma's recommendation."

Clearly, my father does not see what I see in Lauren. Though, come to think of it, I would prefer he did not. The thought of any man looking at her the way I do makes me want to knock someone senseless.

I frown. "Why not?"

"He said I didn't have enough experience. But my friend Ona, who works for his undersecretary, said it's just that I don't have the right pedigree."

Her nose wrinkles and she laughs.

I smile, even without knowing why. "What is so funny?"

"It's just that word pedigree. It's like he was talking about a puppy or something."

She is young enough. That should be reason enough for me to stay away from her. Yet I cannot bring myself to leave.

"If it makes you feel any better, my father did not want me to be the godfather."

"Pedigree problems too?" She winces. "I'm sorry. I just realized that probably isn't something to joke about given . . ."

Her cheeks flush a most appealing shade of pink. I'd love to nibble on them before capturing her mouth in a searing kiss, and—

Shifting in my seat, because I do not want a boner when I am holding my niece.

"It is actually a matter of pedigree. Since the news broke that Sarah will rule instead of me, my father would prefer I stay away and out of the spotlight for another decade or so. At least until people are used to the idea of a future queen."

"Being your niece's godfather puts you in the spotlight?"

"It would seem."

She rolls her eyes. "I'm sorry, but that's silly. You're here to support your family. Not stage a coup."

"Ah, but you see in some people's eyes, that may be precisely why I am here. Or, it could be an invitation for others to meddle in affairs of the crown."

"Sounds pretty far-fetched to me. But what do I know? I'm just an American."

And a beautiful one at that. With her bow-shaped lips upturned toward mine, all I would have to do to taste them is lean forward.

Before I can, the door opens. I jerk back as if I have been caught with my hand in the cookie jar.

My sister enters the room and arches an eyebrow.

"Fancy running into you here."

I rise. "I wanted to get to know my niece. See what the fuss is about."

Sarah's face softens. "Well, I hope you think it is deserved."

"Absolutely," I say, eyes still trained on Lauren. If possible, her face grows even more flushed. So lovely. "Worth every bit of fuss."

LAUREN

The following morning, I open the nursery door to find Prince Henry on the other side. Again. My heart does a little somersault, which I do my best to ignore.

There's no denying it. I'm happy to see him. Even if I'm surprised. The prince spent most of yesterday with Catherine and me, and here he is again. For someone who says he hasn't spent a lot of time around babies, he is an awfully devoted uncle.

"I hope you do not mind," he says with one arm behind his back, "but I brought a little something for the future queen."

He brings his hand forward and reveals a pint-sized plush elephant.

If possible, I melt even more. "She's going to love that."

Henry's eyes wander around the room until they settle on the pram, where Catherine is already nestled.

"Are you getting ready to head out?"

"The princess desires a turn around the garden," I attempt to say in my most posh voice before breaking into a giggle.

"Mind if I join you?"

"By all means."

We circle around the palace's extensive gardens for longer than I originally planned. But Henry and I are so caught up in swapping stories about our lives—and Catherine is cooing happily—I hardly notice how much time has passed. I'm surprised how much we have in common. Who would have guessed a virtual Greek God who is a genuine prince and an aspiring preschool teacher from Idaho would have much in common?

Yet, somehow we do.

I am debating whether or not to turn the corner to prolong our walk when Henry freezes suddenly. His eyes narrow.

Panic slices through me. "What's wrong?"

"Reporters." He gestures to a fence at the end of the garden. I can just spot the lens of a camera poking over the top. "I suppose this will vindicate my father's concerns."

Placing his hand on the small of my back, Henry guides me around a corner behind a hedge. I'm so distracted looking over my shoulder, I trip over a rock. Releasing the pram, I nearly tumble head-first into a fountain.

Strong hands grip my waist. Before I can draw a breath, I'm pulled back up and spun to face Henry. He tears his gaze away from mine for only a moment to pull the pram back over to us.

"Are you alright?" Those bright green eyes are filled with concern.

I nod dumbly. I am suddenly aware of just how hard his body feels pressed against mine. His royal highness clearly makes excellent use of the palace's weight room. Through my cardigan, his hands warm my body.

His eyes flicker to my lips, and I lick them before I can catch myself. Those eyes seem to darken and his face lowers toward mine.

"Your highness!" A voice calls out.

I jump and the top of my head butts into his chin. We pull apart, he rubs his chin, while I clutch the top of my chin.

Around that same hedge, my friend Ona appears. She works as an undersecretary to one of the king's undersecretaries. She's a few years older than me, making her the only palace staff member who understands my dream of a One

Direction reunion as well as my undying love for Taylor Swift.

Her gaze flickers between the prince and I. Eyes lighting up, I know our rapid breaths haven't gone unnoticed by her. My cheeks flush bright red. Great. There is no way I can escape this without getting the third degree.

"Your highness." She curtsies. "Your father has called you to the throne room to review tomorrow's agenda."

Henry rolls his eyes and runs a hand through his dark brown hair. "Wonderful."

Sparing me a glance, he gives a wry grin. "I will see you later?"

I nod, unable to come up with anything intelligible to say. He gives my shoulder a quick squeeze, sending a tingle that radiates through my whole body.

Once we are alone, Ona practically pounces on me.

"So you and the prince?" she wiggles her eyebrows and my cheeks flush all over again. "Nice choice. I mean, he's the only one still on the market, but still, very nice. My sisters and I had crushes on him growing up."

I shake my head. "It's not like that. We're just . . ."

"Friends? With the prince." Ona covers a chuckle. "How many women can say that?"

"Princes need friends too." Though, really, I'm not sure the word friends would describe what's going on between us. "It's not a big deal. He just wanted to spend some time with his niece."

Ona chuckles at that. "Right. I'm sure the prince is super interested in babies."

I wave off her remark and redirect the pram toward the house after making sure Catherine is still content. I give vague responses to Ona's questions and try to ignore her recitation of all the reasons Prince Henry is a catch.

Because I don't need to hear them to know. I could live to be one hundred, and I will never find a man who makes me feel the way I do in his arms.

FOUR

HENRY

I toss to my other side, kicking off some of my covers in the process. After spending most of the past two days with Lauren, I still cannot get her off of my mind. Every time I close my eyes, I see those gold flecks in her eyes and smell the scent of honey and cream that clings to her.

My dick grows even harder. With a grunt of frustration, I toss the covers off of me.

I'll never be able to get to sleep. Not when I know who is tucked away in a bed across the hallway. I glance out my window. It's a clear night. The moon shines brightly over the garden. It's been years since I snuck out of my room at night to roam the palace grounds. Maybe a walk will be just what I need to get a certain someone out of my system.

At the very least, the fresh air will do me some good.

Dressing quickly, I exit through my balcony.

As I walk the gardens, I think about the woman keeping me up. Besides having a body that makes my mouth water,

Lauren has a sharp sense of humor and independence that I find appealing. After years of being fawned over—and having my face plastered over young girls' walls—it's refreshing to spend time with a woman clearly unimpressed by my job.

Both of my brothers mentioned that when they fell for their girlfriends. Alex and James say they like how normal they feel when they are with the women they love.

Is that what is happening to me already?

One thing I do know: I will not be able to deny my need much longer. If Lauren looks at me the way she did earlier today, I am not sure anything will be able to stop me from making her mine.

Maybe I should pay her another visit tomorrow after the christening. Sarah and Ryan already plan to spend the rest of the day with Catherine. I could use the time to whisk Lauren away.

A crunch to my right draws my attention. Lauren steps into view, almost as if I imagined her into reality.

A slow grin spreads across her lips. "I didn't realize I had company."

"I could not sleep."

"Me neither."

We stand there staring at each other. That is when I see it. The spark in her eyes from before. Hell. I cannot ignore it.

Gripping her chin, I turn her face up as my lips lower to hers. The moment our lips meet, sparks shoot through me. My arms move around her body as her hands slide up my chest and around my neck. I urge her mouth open with my tongue. Her own timidly touches mine, and I nearly come undone there.

I need her. Now. But she deserves a little more foreplay.

Pulling back, my chest is rising up and down. I take her

hand and lace my fingers through hers. "Come. I want to show you something."

And after I do, I will make her mine completely.

LAUREN

Henry dives into the pond and resurfaces a moment later. The droplets of water across his skin shimmer in the moonlight. He looks more like a Greek God than ever.

Treading water, he flashes me a grin. "Are you going to come in?"

After Henry kissed me breathless a few moments ago, I was prepared to follow this gorgeous man wherever he led me. But skinny dipping in a pond hidden behind layers of trees and brushes never even crossed my mind.

"No one can see us here." Even from this distance, I can detect the heat in his eyes. "It's just you and me. And I want to see you."

His words nearly make me melt into the earth. They also fill me with confidence I've never had.

Before I can talk myself out of it, I pull the dress over my head and wriggle out of my panties and bra. Glancing over my shoulder to verify that we are in fact alone, I take my first step into the pool and gasp.

"It's cold."

"I'll warm you up."

I wade the rest of the way to him. The water laps at my breast. Between the hungry look in Henry's eyes and the feel of the water against my skin, I am all sensation all over.

Taking my hand, Henry pulls me to his side. The water is too deep for me to stand, but he pulls my legs around his waist and walks me around. I wait for a burst of embarrassment or shyness. It does not come.

Instead, as I gaze into his face, I lean forward for a kiss.

This time, it's even hungrier than before. Earlier it was a taste, now it is a feast. His hands move all over me, leaving tingles behind. I moan into his mouth when his hand brushes the side of my breasts. His thumb flicks my nipple and I almost come right there.

Moving us to shallower water, Henry's head dips down to pull my nipple into his mouth. I gasp as he sucks. He slides a hand between us. I barely have time to brace myself before his fingers find my clit.

Clenching my eyes shut, I cling onto his shoulders. My fingernails dig into his muscles as the tingles of sensation turn into waves of pleasure.

I am only vaguely aware of Henry laying me on the grass at the shore. His mouth lowers from my chest to my abdomen and lower. My eyes flutter open just as his dark head disappears between my thighs. Fingers digging into my ass, he lifts me from the ground and kisses me where his fingers had been moments before.

My breaths become labored as his tongue moves over me and two fingers slide into me. The pressure and pleasure build, mingling together until they burst.

I go limp, wondering how I will ever possibly be able to walk on my own two feet again.

Henry lifts up and comes over me. His mouth meets mine for another intoxicating kiss. I can still taste myself on his lips. "Let me take you to bed. Please?"

As if I could say no.

FIVE

HENRY

Closing the bedroom door behind us, I press Lauren's back against it. My fingers dive into her hair, still wet from our nocturnal swim.

My mouth crashes against hers, urging her lips open so our tongues can duel. Sliding my hands up and down her sides, I trace the curves of her breasts with my thumbs. We must have left her bra down by the pond. They're probably with her shoes. That will make for one hell of a surprise for the gardeners.

She moans into my mouth as I find her nipples. The sounds of her pleasure make me wild with need. I need to feel her—all of her. Sliding my hands down to her hips, I cup her butt and pull her up. Her legs come around my waist, and my cock pushes against the apex of her thighs. She moans again, and I grind against her. The friction of my pants against her panties almost makes me come right there.

Not yet. I want to spill my seed inside her. Thoughts of

letting that seed grow into life, making her round with our child sends a rush of possessiveness through my veins.

I do not just want to make this woman mine in body. I want her to be mine in soul as well. To take care of her. To build a life and a family together. But for now, it is just the two of us. Pledging ourselves to each other with our bodies.

Mine. Ours.

Those words play over and over in my head as I carry her toward the bed. I pull back just enough to pull the dress over her head. I lean her against the covers and inch her panties down her hips, pressing hot, wet kisses along her skin. She wriggles as I do.

I crawl up over her on the bed, cradling my weight on my forearms.

My mouth finds her again as my hands resume their exploration of her body.

Mine. Mine. Mine. And I am hers.

She tears her lips away. "You're wearing too many clothes."

Glancing down at my white shirt, buttoned only halfway up, and my black slacks, I see she is right.

Jumping to my feet again, I toss them aside at record speed and come down upon her again, skin against skin.

My hard cock rubs against her seam. I cannot hold off any longer. Her wetness tickles the tip of my cock. I wonder briefly if I have condoms, then she tells me she is on the pill. She is clean. I am clean. Now it is time to truly make her mine.

I take one of her nipples into my mouth, and her back arches up. Using that movement, I release her and flip onto my back, bringing her over me.

With her legs straddling my hips, I grip onto her hands as

she slowly eases onto me. Inch by inch, I fill her pussy. I clench my eyes shut.

"You are so tight."

Then she moves forward and I hiss through my teeth. My fingers dig into her skin as I urge her in riding me. Hot lava runs through my veins. I want her to come again. To come around me. I move one of my thumbs to her front, finding her clit. My thumb makes circles around her, and she cries out my name.

Our breaths increase, my heart pounds in my ears.

And when I am not sure I can hold on much longer, she quivers around me. Her pleasure grabs onto my own. They mix together, pulsing in and out of each other until we fall apart and over the edge into blissful oblivion.

She collapses against my chest, and I wrap my arms around her.

A few minutes later, when I can speak properly, I glance down at her. "I would like to take you out for a proper date tomorrow night."

Those sweet lips of hers, still swollen from mine, curve into a smile that nearly stops my heart.

SIX

LAUREN

I am standing in front of the mirror debating which of two dresses I should wear for my date with Henry this evening when there is a knock at the door.

Looking at the time, I frown. The family should all be en route to the cathedral by now. Not that I've seen any of them since Henry slipped out of my bed this morning.

Tossing the dresses on my bed, I throw the door open and smile at Ona, who is carrying a pile of newspapers.

"Oh perfect. I could use a second opinion." I reach for the dresses and hold them up. "Which one should I go with?"

Ona closes the door slowly behind her.

"I am afraid I am the bearer of bad news."

I freeze. "What's wrong? Is anyone hurt?"

"On behalf of the secretary to the king of Rhodon, I must inform you that your services are no longer required." Ona's eyes take a frosty tint. "Your termination is effective immediately."

My heart drops to my feet. "Why?"

Ona holds up the newspapers. It takes me a moment to realize what I'm looking at. When I do, my heart stops beating altogether.

There, in full color is my virtually naked body. In each picture, I'm kissing Henry in the pond. I burn with embarrassment remembering what happened just a few minutes after they were taken. That was just last night. How can there be pictures in a paper this morning?

"Are there any other pictures?"

"I think we both know there are. Fortunately, for your sake, they were too scandalous for publication."

I am such a freaking idiot. I know Henry said the pond was private, but someone clearly followed us. A moment that had been just ours is now on display for the world to see. Bile rises in my throat.

Once these photos hit the international news cycle, there won't be a school district in the world that will give me a job.

I'm spiraling into a pit of outrage, despair, and humiliation when the headlines on the papers come into focus.

Royal Nanny Getting Busy with Mystery Man
Bare Noble Rumored to be the Duke of Orkhis

"Why would anyone think that's the duke and me?"

"Because it's the story the papers were fed."

"But who . . ." That's when it hits me. "It was you."

"I had a job to do." Ona's face remains stern. "It is unfortunate you were caught in the crosshairs, but it was necessary. Of course, when we originally devised the plan, we hoped the duke would in fact stray for the beautiful, young nanny. But he never looks anywhere but the princess. So, we had to be creative."

My eyes return to the paper, where my virtually naked

body is there for everyone to see. "What could you possibly think you're going to accomplish by starting a rumor that the Duke and I are having an affair?"

"It is obvious to everyone who knows anything that the princess is crumbling under the pressure."

"You hope this news will break her?"

Ona gives a short nod. "Everyone in the know understands she will put saving her marriage above the crown. She'll abdicate. Henry will step back into the role that should have been his all along."

I shake my head. "You're staging a coup."

"We're righting a wrong."

Henry was right. Though it had seemed impossible to me, some people will stop at nothing to keep a man on the throne.

"The only thing wrong is your backward thinking." I throw the papers on the floor just as there's another knock on the door. "I assume that is the royal guard here to escort me out of the palace?"

"You have ten minutes to get your things." Ona folds her arms across her chest. "It's nothing personal. But the royals had to be protected."

"They do need protection. From you."

There are at least a dozen other choice things I'd like to say to her, but the guards are now in the room, and I need to pack. As I pull out my suitcase, my heart aches. My whole world is falling apart. I won't even get a chance to say goodbye to Henry.

The possibility that he might come to find me flashes through my head briefly, but I dismiss it. No, regardless of the pull that drew us together, Henry is honorable above all things. He will stay to help his family and sister.

Maybe, someday, when all this blows over we can be together. I tell myself that even as I know it will never happen.

SEVEN

HENRY

Someone in the palace is going to be sent packing. I may not have much influence around the place anymore if I ever did. But after seeing such an intimate moment between Lauren and I plastered over the Internet, I will use whatever pull I have to get to the bottom of this.

Either we have someone selling family secrets to the press inside the palace, or we have someone giving the press unauthorized access to our family. Regardless, we have a traitor on staff, and they should be sacked.

Poor Lauren must be beside herself. I did not have a chance to see her before I left the palace for the cathedral. It was only after I was in the car and saw the photos that I realized I do not even have her number to send her a quick text. I nearly turned the car around, but I am fairly certain my father would replace me as godfather if I were to arrive even a moment late for the service.

I cannot let my sister down today. Especially not when I

am the nude backside being labeled as her husband's all over the Internet.

How anyone could believe Ryan would cheat on Sarah is beyond me.

I barely have time to say hello to my sister, who just whispers she needs to speak with me after the service. She looks worried, but not sad or angry, which I take as a good sign. Though I try my best to pay attention to the words the priest says, I find my mind wandering to Lauren. I hope she is not too upset. We can get through it. Together.

We barely finish the processional out of the sanctuary when Sarah grabs me by the arm and tugs me into a room. Ryan, who is holding Catherine, closes the door behind us.

"Before you say anything, it was me in the photos. And I will get to the bottom of this."

She blinks at me in surprise. "Of course I know it was you. I could spot any of my brothers—not to mention my husband—in a line-up front, backward, or upside down."

"I am still sorry it broke today. I am going to find the mole."

"We already know who it is." Sarah frowns. "One of our father's undersecretaries is apparently a hold-out from the previous administration who . . ."

"Who falsified our birth order on the records."

"Precisely. And the undersecretary had his under-secretary—"

"There are too many damn undersecretaries if you ask me," Ryan mutters.

"Is the one who took and sold the photo." Sarah shakes her head. "Both of them will be fired by the time we finish lunch."

"Oh." A weight lifts from my shoulders. "Thank you for taking care of that so quickly."

"Not so fast. There is still the matter of Lauren."

"What about her?" Wait a moment. "Do not tell me you disapprove. You married your—"

"Of course I do not disapprove. You are both consenting adults." She rolls her eyes at me. "However, father says they fired Lauren this morning."

It is like a punch to the gut. "Is she okay?"

Sarah shakes her head. "I wish I knew."

My jaw tightens. "If you do not mind, I think I might skip the luncheon."

"There is a car waiting for you out front."

I press a quick kiss to her cheek and Catherine's head, then I am out the door. I wonder if I still have any contacts in the aviation security office who can find out what flight Lauren is taking. With any luck, she is still here in the country. I can meet her at the airport. Otherwise, I will be on the next plane out—wherever she is going.

A few feet away from the car, a small pack of journalists appears. They thrust microphones in my face.

"How is the princess taking the news of the alleged affair?"

"Did you have any idea your brother-in-law could be a two-timer?"

"How has this affected your niece's christening?"

"Will the king make an official statement?"

Really, they should all know that no member of the royal family will respond to gossip. I nearly slam the door on their questions to illustrate the point but freeze.

Wherever she is, Lauren might see this. To hell with royal protocol.

"Actually, I would like to make a statement of my own if I might." Stepping back out of the car, I stand tall, straightening my suit jacket. "The photos published earlier today are of myself and a young woman I am seeing. Regrettably, someone in our household violated a private moment between us. Just like it is regrettable those photos were used to frame my brother-in-law for something he would never do."

My jaw ticks. "The men in my family are fiercely protective of the women we love. We would never do anything to intentionally hurt them. I am sorry for any pain this caused my sister, her family, and the woman in the pictures. I hope the press will do the right thing and stop promoting the images and the lies around them."

The reporters stand in stunned silence for another moment. Then the questions start up again.

"Can you confirm the woman's identity?"

"Is this serious or is it a fling?"

"What can you tell us about the person who leaked the story?"

I give a stern look to the press corps and they fall silent.

"I will leave any statements about the leak to the palace." I swallow hard. "Out of respect for the woman in the pictures, I will not confirm, deny, or clarify her identity. I will also not share specifics about our relationship. But a word of advice to you all."

They remain silent, hanging on to each of my words. Suckers.

"I would be respectful of her going forward. I intend to have her at my side for at least the next fifty years or so."

EIGHT

LAUREN

I am standing in the airport lobby staring at a TV screen, my jaw wide open. Did Prince Henry, the man who has completely captured my heart, just tell the world he wants to spend the rest of his life with me?

It's almost enough to wipe away the pain and humiliation of the rest of the day.

It's almost enough to make me want to call a taxi and have it take me back to the palace. To bang on the door until they let me in to see him. To risk being thrown back out in the streets.

It's definitely enough to give me hope that he will give me a call using the phone number I managed to sneak under his door before I was escorted out of the palace hours ago.

Still virtually paralyzed with shock, it takes me almost a full minute to realize a familiar voice is calling my name. I turn in time to see Henry sprint across the lobby.

"Oh thank God you have not left already." He wraps his

arms around me. "I do not have enough words to tell you how sorry I am."

"It wasn't your fault."

"I should have protected you better." His arms tighten around me. "I will protect you better in the future."

Then he pulls back suddenly. " Lauren, there is something I must ask you."

He begins to lower to one knee, but I grab his arms before he can.

"But the pictures of me." I shake my head like that will somehow knock the images out of my head. "I'm basically naked on the cover of every paper in Europe. And half the ones back home."

"For what it's worth"—He wraps his arms around me and strokes my back—"you look fucking hot in those pictures."

I gasp and push away from him. "That's such a Man thing to say."

Henry loosens his hold but doesn't let go of me completely.

"I do not mean to undermine the seriousness of the situation." The sincerity on his face lessens some of my irritation. "Someone betrayed your trust and sold you out to advance a bogus political agenda."

Then his eyes narrow. He looks mad enough to punch someone. And, unfortunately, there are way too many interested eyes with camera phones pointed at us to risk a fistfight with a stranger.

"It's okay," I assure him.

"It is not. We will get to the bottom of this." His jaw tightens. "In the meantime, she has been fired. And we have the option to file charges."

My eyes widen. "You would file charges?"

"Of course." His gaze softens then. "I meant what I said

in that interview. You are my present and my future. I love you."

My heart flutters. Even as I start to imagine spending the rest of my life with him, and maybe a couple of kids of our own along the way, I can't get ahead of myself.

"I love you too."

Just saying those words makes them feel even more true. I love him. And I love being able to say that.

Henry's lips break into a grin and lower to mine. I press a hand against his chest to hold him back.

"How will this work?" I gesture to our audience, their phones still focused on us.

"Hmm, I see what you mean." He nods. "Well, what would you like? I can renounce my title and we can move to Idaho or wherever you want to live."

My stomach drops. "You'd give up your family for me?"

"We will of course have to pop around for the occasional wedding and christening, but as for being a working member of the royal family?" He lifts a shoulder. "I would give all that up for you in a heartbeat."

"But the king?"

Henry just lifts a shoulder. "So what do you say? Shall we run away together?"

"We could." I trace the lapel of his jacket with my fingertips. "But neither of us are really the run from trouble types."

He arches an eyebrow. "Are you suggesting . . . ?"

"Wouldn't it be more interesting to plant some roots here in Rhodon?"

"It would." A slow grin spreads across that handsome face of his. "Especially if we make a big splash with a big community service project."

That sends a new thrill through me. "I'm listening."

"And I have ideas about that to discuss with you, but first

things first. Lauren, love of my life, I hope you will do me the honor of sticking with me through it all."

"Till death do us part?"

"Through thick and thin."

"I will." Then I lean up on my toes to seal that promise with a kiss.

Cameras around us flash. I'll have to get used to that if I am serious about taking on this man and his baggage. And I am. Because a love like this is worth it. Besides. It's easy to forget about cameras—and everything else in the world—when he's kissing me.

I'll just have to spend the next fifty or sixty years kissing him all the time. That's a pretty good way to spend the rest of my life.

EPILOGUE

LAUREN

one year later

All around me, cameras flash while journalists with microphones elbow each other to get to the front of the crowd. My hands are shaking as I grip onto the oversized pair of scissors.

Then, Henry arrives at my side and places a gentle hand to the small of my back.

"Okay?" he asks through a bright smile while waving to the crowd of journalists and spectators.

I suck in a breath and nod. "I will be."

"It's your first official appearance as a full-fledged member of the royal family."

I glance down at my still shaking hands and catch the glitter of light from the oversized emerald and matching band. Seeing both, I can't help but grin. Henry had given me the engagement ring just a week after Catherine's christening.

We waited almost a year to get married. Not because either of us had cold feet. But I really wanted to finish the last year of my master's degree in early childhood development. And Henry, always wanting to see me happy, agreed to set our wedding date for two weeks after my graduation.

By the time our wedding rolled around, I half expected royal watchers worldwide—let alone in Rhodon—to be over weddings. What with all four of the king's children tying the knot in such quick succession.

Instead, all four siblings—two pairs of twins—marrying so close together seemed to add even more hype. I'm sure it didn't hurt that all of their spouses were American.

While the King of Rhodon had been less than thrilled to see all four of his children marry title-less Americans, he enjoyed the good publicity it gave him and the whole family.

And now they are my family. It still seems impossible. Like I will wake up one day and Henry won't be lying next to me in bed, and I'll realize it was all a dream.

Because I am living a dream.

Even if facing a loud crowd of people trying to get my picture feels a bit like a nightmare.

Henry's hand gently caresses my back, reminding me that we're in this together. We really are on this particular project of ours.

With a parting squeeze to my shoulder, Henry steps toward the microphone.

"Creating opportunities for future generations of Rhodonians is a cause my wife and I are particularly passionate about. It is with great pleasure that we open the Rhodon Center for Child Development and Discovery."

Henry turns to flash me a grin, and I nearly melt into the floor. I will never, ever get used to this handsome, charming husband of mine.

"My wife and I are committed to seeing this center prosper, which is why she will be teaching in one of the classrooms, and I will work with the administrators."

There's a murmur of excitement throughout the crowd.

"We would like to thank the people of Rhodon, my father the king, and particularly my sister, the Crowned Princess Sarah who helped to make today possible." His jaw sets as he looks out. "We will not let you down."

He steps away from the microphone. While applause thunders around us, he returns to my side. My hands are steady as he covers them with his own.

"Ready?"

I nod. Together we cut the ribbon to our passion project. We share a glance and a smile. The past year has been a whirlwind. I would bet the next fifty will be just as chaotic. But as long as I have Henry and he has me, we'll keep each other steady and grounded.

BONUS EPILOGUE

HENRY

twenty years later

"Long live the queen."

Lauren raises her contraband glass of champagne to clink with mine. Technically the toasts are supposed to come after the coronation of Queen Sarah of Rhodon, but we have a lot to celebrate.

It has been a year since my father, the King of Rhodon died. While we had a complicated relationship, I am grateful that in his final years, he seemed to mellow. He made time to enjoy his sixteen grandchildren. And while I am not sure he ever entirely came around to liking that all four of his children married fiercely independent and ambitious Americans, he at least gave us all his blessing.

In the end, all four of his children were at his side when he peacefully passed away. In the end, he knew that no matter what had happened in the past, his children loved him and he loved us.

While we and the nation mourned, we also carried on. It was what our father had ingrained in all of us. A sense of duty to the people of Rhodon. I see now how lucky we are to also have somehow learned a sense of family and unity. If we were close as children, we are thick as thieves now.

Particularly on my sister's coronation day.

"A toast," I say, after we swallow our first sips of champagne, "to my intelligent, beautiful wife, the Duchess of Kryos. The woman who has grown one early childhood development center to a whole network, now making Rhodon a world leader in education."

She grins as we drink. Then, Lauren raises her glass once more.

"To my husband, the new minister of state."

Though my father had come around to much later in his life, he never had believed his children should be more than public figures. I am fortunate my sister thinks otherwise.

"To our children."

All four of them—Stella, Jasper, Asher, and Nora—are down the hallway with Sarah's children. With the queen and her prince regent set to arrive last for the ceremony, Lauren and I have the honor of escorting two pre-teens, four teenagers, and two college students home on vacation to the cathedral.

If we get there without any of the siblings picking fights with each other, and no one pouting, I am fairly certain my sister will give me a medal.

"To twenty years of marriage." I slip an arm around my wife's waist and pull her close. "To being even more in love with you today than when I married you."

With champagne still bubbling on our tongues, our mouths collide in a kiss that leaves us even dizzier than a glass of champagne at eight in the morning.

I trace the curve of my wife's bottom through her satin dress, earning a giggle and a swat.

"Don't even think about it." But her eyes sparkle in delight. "Do you know how long it took to press the wrinkles out of this dress?"

"That is a shame." And it is because I am just as wild with need for her now as I was when we first met. "Willing to see if it is worth a few wrinkles?"

My wife just laughs at me and finishes off her glass of champagne. Hand in hand, we step out of the room to continue the celebration with our family and kingdom.

We both have our duties today and our purpose in life. It is all I ever wanted.

BONUS EPILOGUE

JAMES

"What are you doing?"

I freeze. I am in the middle of tucking a copy of my wife's latest novel into the tote bags the queen will be giving to all of her guests at the coronation. It was supposed to be a surprise. Only she has caught me in the act.

Dropping the book and stepping away from the bags, I lift a shoulder. "Nothing."

"It doesn't look like nothing." Alyssa glides into the room, her silk gown rustling as she does. "Were you stealing from the swag bags?"

"Of course not."

Like I would ever need to steal anything. Between Alyssa's two-decade career as a best-selling author and my skills as a leading investor and economist, I could afford to buy hundreds of her books.

Which is precisely what I have done. Only, again, she was not supposed to find out just yet.

Hands on her hips, Alyssa frowns at me. "Spill. Or I will call a guard in to shake you down."

Sighing, I reach into a box and hand her one of the books.

Her eyes widen. "What are you doing with these?"

"It is the first of your books with your real name on the cover. I want everyone I know to have a copy."

My wife created quite a stir in the literary community—and beyond—when she announced last month that she was the author behind dozens of best-selling romance novels.

"So you're giving one away to everyone who comes to the coronation ball?"

I shrug. "Everyone could do with a little more reading."

Alyssa's eyes crinkle around the edges as she laughs. Heat licks the back of my neck, and I turn to leave the room when my wife throws her arms around me, stopping me in my track.

"You, the Duke of Paion, will never cease to amaze and surprise me." She squeezes me until I'm nearly out of breath. "And I love you and this crazy life we have."

I bring my arms around her, resting my chin against the crown of her head.

"You do not mind that we are staying here on a more permanent basis then?"

Her head moves beneath my chin. "You can make real change as the minister of finance. Plus, the kids like being closer to their cousins."

It is true. Our children Seth, Harriet, Jacob, and Tyler have already adapted well to their schools.

"Besides," she arches her neck to press a kiss to my chin. "Where better to get inspiration for my next novel then right here?"

"About that, I have a few ideas for one of your sexier scenes."

"I'll look forward to acting it out with you tonight in bed."

BONUS EPILOGUE

ALEX

The kids are dressed and pressed for the coronation, but according to the driver, my wife has disappeared.

Fortunately, after more than twenty years of marriage, I know where to find her.

Taking the back stairway down from the three-story flat we renovated years ago, I find Nikki in the kitchen of her flagship bakery. Dressed in satin and tulle, she has an apron over her gown as she carefully touches up the buttercream on the cake.

Even though we are about to be late, I keep my mouth shut. If more than twenty years of marriage has taught me anything, it is to never interrupt my wife when she is in the middle of creating one of her masterpieces. Especially when that masterpiece will be at the coronation ball.

Besides, it gives me a rare chance to just observe her. With her tongue sticking out of her full lips, and her cobalt blue eyes focused on the piping, she is every bit as gorgeous as she was when I met her. I still want to lick that frosting off of her just as much.

We do not have as much time as we once did to sneak away to the bakery for fun with baked goods. With four children—Sophia, Holden, Joshua, and Trevor—a franchise with more than fifty bakery locations worldwide, and a country to guard and protect, we are pretty busy.

But every so often, I will get a message from my wife that she has leftover chocolate sauce or buttercream. She will ask if I would like to lick the bowl.

The answer is always yes.

My wife's eyes glance up then. Catching my stare, a slow grin spreads across her lips.

"Unfortunately I don't have a bowl for you to lick today."

"If you did, there is no time to do it properly." I move behind her and wrap my arms around her waist.

"What do you think?"

"Another masterpiece." Like always. I pull the strawberry blonde curls from her neck and kiss the smooth skin. Goosebumps pop up on her skin. I love that I still have this kind of reaction on her.

She sighs, and I am momentarily tempted to make us very late to the coronation.

Seemingly reading my thoughts, Nikki gives a low, sultry chuckle. It has the same effect as if she reached around and stroked my cock.

"I think it would look bad if the Duke and Duchess of Anemone were late for the procession." She sets the piping aside and turns in my arms. "Besides, my hands are sticky. I can't go and get frosting in the minister of defense's hair."

"Pity." I brush my lips across hers, not wanting to smudge her lipstick. "Pick up where we left off tonight?"

Her lips curl up. "As it happens, I do have extra butter-cream in the fridge."

"I know just where to put it."

SARAH

Meeting me outside the waiting room in the cathedral, Ryan lets out a low whistle.

"Babe, you're stunning." He presses his lips to my bare shoulder and lowers his voice. "If the place wasn't crawling with servants, and you didn't have a billion viewers around the world waiting for you to appear, I'd fuck you right now."

I giggle. "You cannot say that. We are in a church."

"Doesn't that make it more exciting?"

I roll my eyes, pretending to be annoyed. But how can I be? What woman does not enjoy being irresistible to her husband even after more than twenty years of marriage? Not even a queen—or, rather, almost queen—is above that.

"I am a little nervous," I whisper.

"Don't be. Just put one foot in front of the other."

It sounds so simple. "Take it a step at a time?"

"That's right." He grins. "Besides you'll have your brothers, their families, our children, and me here every step of the way."

He gestures down the hallway, where sure enough my brothers, their wives, and their children are all lined up to begin the processional. Our children—Catherine, Alexis, and the twins Harrison and Jameson—are with them. Though we have faced ups and downs and plenty of in-betweens in our lives together, we have been united. Not just as a dynasty, but as a family.

Through every bit of it, I have relied on the strong, handsome man standing next to me. With dashing streaks of gray at his temples, I would marry Ryan again today if I could.

A single tear slips down my cheek as my heart fills.

"Hey." Ryan brushes a thumb across my cheek. "We can't have the queen crying on her coronation day."

Then he kisses me just below my ear, sending a shiver of delight through me. Now I wish we had about twenty minutes to sneak off to find a closet.

The bronze doors swing open. My brothers and the other nobles lead the procession down the aisle. Ryan offers me his arm and I take it.

My reign as queen of Rhodon will officially begin the next time I step through those doors. I hope I will be a good and just leader and guide my country with kindness and grace. Whatever happens during this chapter in Rhodon's history, I know it will be filled with love and hope.

It will be better than any happily ever after in any fairy tale. And it belongs to all of us.

Want more royal romances? Check out *Peanut Brittle and the Prince.*

Click here to receive a FREE sweet and steamy instalove romance short read.

For updates on new and upcoming releases, follow me on BookBub, and connect with me on Facebook, Instagram, TikTok, and YouTube.

Visit my merch shop for T-shirts, mugs, and more.

Curvy Girls Bucket List
Firth Mountain Smokejumpers
A Short, Sweet, and Steamy Christmas